THE ANGELS' SHARE

Laurence Shames

The Angels' Share
by Laurence Shames
First Print Edition
Copyright © 2012 by Laurence Shames
http://www.laurenceshames.com
ISBN-13: 978-15059709-7-5
ISBN-10: 1505970970

To Marilyn

"All goes onward and outward, nothing collapses,
And to die is different from what any one supposed, and luckier."
– Walt Whitman

"There wasn't a lot of bullshit in my heaven."
– Alice Sebold

Part I

The Kissing Corner

1.

At Cottage Hospital in Santa Barbara, California, there is an intersection of hallways known as kissing corner. It is the place where gurneys pause to allow patients and their loved ones a last moment together before the terrifying adventure of surgery.

On any given day, a couple of dozen little dramas play out at kissing corner. Sometimes there are prayers; sometimes there are tears. Sometimes there are dark and seldom funny jokes aimed at beating back fear with mockery. Often the exchanges are utterly mundane—a reminder to pick up the dry cleaning, to put out fresh milk for the cat. This, too, is a stratagem for keeping fear at bay; a pretended certainty that all will be well and life, just a day or two from now, will go on as it always has.

There are the final hugs, embraces made clumsy by the need to dodge I.V. poles and tubes and dangling jars of mysterious liquids. Foreheads are stroked, brave smiles attempted over teeth that have gone dry. Then the orderly, clad in mint-green scrubs, decides that the moment is over. He pushes the gurney forward, negotiating a turn that is never quite crisp, but has an element of sideways slipping, like a sailboat making leeway. Brushed steel doors swing apart, and the patient vanishes, soon to be cut open.

Almost always, the loved one lingers a long moment in the hallway, staring at the now closed doors, as if expecting that some embarrassing mistake has been made and will any second be rectified. The spouse or parent or sibling or friend is not really so ill and does not need an operation; he or she will surely be rolled out again, sitting up and smiling. This daydream endures for several breaths and then dissolves. The loved one walks away and wonders where to spend the next few hours.

It is, again, a common drama. It could not be otherwise, for in our troubles we are all the same. Our victories belong to us alone—or so we like to think; but our frailties and our tragedies are universal. We are fellow-travelers in sickness and in loss. We are comrades and compatriots in regret. We are equal, and equally helpless, in the face of all the things that can happen to us.

At the same time, we are unique in what we do. We make choices to the humbling extent that they are ours to make; a trick of focus helps us think of this as freedom. The choices, strung together, make our lives our own and no one else's. They define us in our own skin and in regard to others. They determine how or if we love, and how or if we are loved in return.

That is why, for all their common threads, no two partings at kissing corner are precisely the same. The words may be alike; the ritual gestures are familiar. But each goodbye carries within it an impossibly dense summation of a unique relationship. Old aches, resentments, yearnings. Questions that were never asked, or never answered, or the answers never understood. The million things that might have been different. All of these crowd into a moment that will inevitably feel inadequate and rushed. There is more to say than can possibly be said, and this brief conversation in a hospital hallway might be the very last chance to say it. This is far too much pressure to put on a moment. Since the moment can't be stretched indefinitely, there is a contrary impulse just to get it over with. Partings at kissing corner, however long they last, always end up feeling awkwardly abrupt.

On a particular morning one early spring, a young woman was walking beside her father's gurney as it was being wheeled to kissing corner. She was tall and trim, with suntanned skin and slender strands of muscle earned by long habits of swimming in the surf and running on the beach. She seemed unaccustomed to walking as slowly as was now required; even so, there was an unself-conscious grace in how she moved, an alert and robust forward tilt to her shoulders. Her name was Darcy Barnett. She was twenty-nine years old and couldn't remember ever being in a hospital before.

She strolled, listening to the wheels click softly over the seams in the tile floor. At some point her father reached out and took her wrist. He held it gently; even so, she felt herself recoil slightly. Her father had an intravenous line pegged into the back of his hand; she couldn't help finding this spooky. Besides, it had been a long time since she'd been entirely comfortable being touched by her father.

Turning his head against the pillow, blinking up at the fluorescent lights, he said to Darcy, "I'm glad you're here."

"Mom would have wanted me to be."

It was a grudging answer and was meant as such. He wished she'd said something else. Secretly, she wished it, too; but long habits were hard to break, and the habits that pertained between members of failed families were among the hardest of all.

Putting aside his disappointment, he said, "When I get out of here, let's have a nice dinner somewhere."

"Only if you don't sneak outside to smoke." This was meant as humor but came out as reproach.

Hugh Barnett pressed his lips together and looked up at his daughter. In some ways they resembled one another; in other ways not at all. Hugh was handsome, but his good looks were of the sort that were apparent in the first glance and took on a certain blandness over time. His eyes were dark and deep-set. His nose was straight, with a slight flattening of the bridge that gave an impression of ruggedness. He had a square chin, beautiful teeth, a full head of mostly silver hair—all very regular and standard. Darcy's beauty was more complicated, a matter of moods and facets that only gradually became compelling. She had curly and luxuriant reddish-brown hair that tended to spill in corkscrews down across her forehead; sometimes her hair seemed to tumble down from sheer exuberance, other times it seemed more like a curtain she could hide behind. Her eyes were hazel mixed with glints of green; even when she smiled, they turned down just slightly at the outside corners, suggesting something darker mixed in with the amusement.

The gurney rolled. The wheels clicked. Finally Darcy's father managed half a protest, half an apology. "What can I say? I've tried to quit. A dozen times. I have to smoke. I'm addicted. I don't think you understand."

She moved her chin a few degrees away, as though she wasn't really talking to her father. "Oh but I do."

He might have followed up on that, but didn't. He said, "We'll take a ride up to Ojai. Go out to the Ranch House. How's that?"

"Just get better first, okay?"

If the intention was tender, the tone was not. The patient looked sideways at his daughter. As the gurney was approaching kissing corner, he said, "Darcy, I'm a little scared."

"You'll be fine. I know you will. You don't even look sick."

"I don't?"

"Not much. Not really."

"I want things to be better between you and me."

"Not the best time to discuss it, Dad. But we'll work on it, okay?"

"Promise?"

"Promise."

The orderly had moved a discreet step or two away. Darcy reached down and stroked her father's hair. Touching him made her fingers feel brittle. She tried to smile. He tried to smile back.

The man in the mint-green scrubs moved to the head of the gurney. A heartbeat too late, the patient said, "I love you, baby." The words were lost in the squeaks and bumps of the wheels against the floor.

2.

Darcy watched the brushed steel doors close behind her father. She lingered a few moments to see if he would be rolled out again, as if this whole surgery business had been some crazy and grotesque mistake. When that didn't happen, she began to walk away.

She'd taken several steps before she realized she had no idea where she was going next. Suddenly shaky, burdened by the many things that had not been said, she couldn't quite remember the sequence of hallways that would take her out of the hospital. She was upset with herself for not managing to be kinder to her father, not managing to rise above the thought that he didn't really deserve her kindness.

Somehow she found her way out to the street. It was still quite early in the morning. Off to the south, over the ocean, a light fog shimmered. On the inland side, the hills, mottled green from the winter rains, gleamed in dry, yellow light. Huge ficus trees grew between the sidewalks and the roadways; their waxy leaves always looked freshly washed and polished.

Out in the sunshine, walking at a clip brisk enough to put a tingle in her calves, she soon felt better, though there were a few preoccupations she could not outpace. Her father was going in to surgery. In truth, she wasn't panicked; she saw his operation as a worry but not a crisis. She knew he'd be okay. He'd recover, probably go back to smoking. Smoking, she was sure, would kill him eventually. Just not now. It couldn't happen now, in part at least because father and daughter still had much to figure out together.

That thought flowed seamlessly into another of her preoccupations—the fact that she would soon be turning thirty. She hadn't expected this to bother her, but lately it did, and she was struggling to understand why. She considered herself a happy person. She had a career, friends, a congenial place to live; her life was pretty well on track. True, she had some issues; didn't everyone? Hers mostly had to do with trust. Trust in men, specifically, and specifically where romance was involved. When it came to romance, she'd always had a hard time believing that anything would last. Mistrusting her partners, she'd mistrusted herself as well. She'd always needed to allow herself an out, to see a line of daylight at the bottom of the exit door. She'd tended to storm through relationships in a series of spasms; quick to fall in love, quick to doubt, and quick to pull the plug. She would rather throw something away than wait around to lose it.

She knew all this about herself. In her twenties, it didn't seem to matter very much. People came and went. There were thrills and letdowns, fleeting euphoria and fleeting heartbreak. Wasn't that what one's twenties were for?

But now that decade was ending, and Darcy was being nagged by the sense that she didn't want her life to be that way forever. She was bothered by something else as well. When she'd thought about it at all, she used to imagine that her problems with trust would be resolved by time, that she'd simply outgrow them, like a childhood lisp. Now she knew it wouldn't happen that way. It would take work. It would require tracking the mistrust back to its source.

This, of course, brought her thoughts once again to the man being wheeled into surgery—her handsome, charming, dishonest, philandering father. She loved him, she hated him. She adored him, she blamed him. She needed to understand him better. Walking quickly through the beautiful streets of Santa Barbara, she decided that once he was out of the hospital she would try to see more of him, talk things through, get to know him as a grown-up instead of as a wounded little girl. She promised herself that she would really, really try.

The prep room smelled of rubbing alcohol and green soap.

Anesthesiologists and surgeons shuffled around in paper booties and paper hats that looked like bouffant shower caps. Hugh Barnett, awaiting his turn in the operating room, had been rolled into a space between two curtains that hung in pleats from curving rods.

A relentlessly cheerful nurse came over to confirm his name and date of birth. Doing the math, she said, "You're sixty-eight?"

He nodded that he was.

"That's young these days."

"You're telling me," he said.

She asked him what procedure he was there to have. He said, "Carotid endarter—"

"Endarterectomy," said the nurse. "You got farther than most. One side or both?"

"Both."

She looked down at a chart. "Good. We agree on that." She bent low over him so that her body blotted out the light, and, with a felt-tip pen, drew small *x*'s on both sides of his neck.

"Magic marker? You write on me with magic marker?"

"Sometimes low-tech is still the best. Your symptoms—any change since you last spoke with Dr. Singh?"

"Not really," said Barnett. In this he was lying, though he didn't quite know it. Decades of nicotine had stiffened and shrunk his arteries, and blood was stalling in his silted-up passages; in recent weeks, he'd been prone to a subtle sort of dizziness. Light would swim at the edges of his vision if he turned his head too quickly; there was a faint humming in his ears, soft but deep and resonant, like a whale song. His failure to acknowledge his worsening condition could easily be called denial; equally, however, it could be ascribed to a merciful tendency for sick people not to accurately register every creeping increment of getting sicker.

The nurse said, "You're aware of the risks of the procedure?"

He nodded that he was. Carotid endarterectomies were fairly routine surgeries, but since they involved an interruption of blood flow to the brain, things could always go wrong. The artery on one side of the neck was bypassed with a catheter so that it could be sliced open, scraped free of plaque, and stitched together once again. Then the process was repeated on the other side. But sometimes the catheters clogged. Or the artery that remained open proved too hard and narrow to satisfy the brain's appetite for oxygen, and cells would start to die, taking with them packets of memory, control of muscles, use of language. Or a tiny bit of plaque—a particle not much larger than a dust mote—could break free and lodge, by merest chance, in some unlucky spot, damming up a capillary that would swell and throb and finally burst in a minuscule but catastrophic flood.

Hugh Barnett said, "I have a living will. You have that in your papers, right?"

The nurse riffled through a few sheets on her clipboard until she found it.

He said, "If it's dicey, if it's a judgment call, don't wake me up."

"It'll be fine. Dr. Singh has done hundreds of these."

The patient clenched and unclenched the hand without the I.V. line. He'd gone to the limit of what he'd let himself think about. Now he stepped back to the everyday, the trivial. "How long's the operation?"

The cheerful nurse said, "Why? You have a date?"

"Maybe. What time you get off?"

"Ah," she said, "a Romeo. My favorite kind of patient." She stuck a probe in his ear to take his temperature.

3.

Darcy walked for three-quarters of an hour, then felt an irresistible need to get back to the hospital. There was absolutely nothing she could do there; perversely, this sense of helplessness only added to her desire to sit nearby, to keep the vigil, to put in the time.

She found the waiting room for people with loved ones in surgery. She gave her name and her father's name to a volunteer who dispensed peppermints and soothing words. Then she sat down near a very old man who had suspenders on; his pants gapped out from his shrunken waist. Across from her, a woman worked on a laptop. Members of a Mexican family shuttled in and out.

She riffled through a magazine. She didn't read it; she couldn't concentrate. After a while, a young man came in and went to the volunteer desk to register. Darcy glanced at him as abstractedly as she had looked at the magazine. He wore jeans and a light blue shirt. He was tall. He had short hair that was so black it was almost blue.

That was all she noticed—until she saw an odd detail that focused her attention. His fingertips were stained a garnet color—not quite red, not quite orange, not quite pink. His fingernails looked opalescent, framed as they were by the almost ruby cuticles.

He turned away from the volunteer desk. His eyes met Darcy's very briefly and they exchanged polite nods and sympathetic smiles. The tall man sat down nearby, leaving an empty chair between them.

But Darcy could not stop glancing over at his garnet fingertips, and after a few moments he felt the gaze. Splaying out his fingers, he said, "Been scrubbing barrels." He lifted his chin toward the waiting room doorway. "You have somebody here?"

"My father. Getting some arteries reamed out. You?"

"My mom. Hip replacement."

She looked at him more closely. His eyes, a surprising combination with the jet black hair, were the same light blue as his shirt. His nose was straight and broad. His shoulders and chest were wide but not bulky. Rawboned was the word that came to mind.

He said, "You and your Dad. You close?"

Darcy came out with a sound that started as an unmirthful laugh but then caught in her throat. "Close? No. He left. Long time ago. You close with your mom?"

"Yeah. Pretty close. She's widowed, I'm an only child."

"Me too. Only child, I mean. Dad has no one else."

The young man gave an accepting shrug; or at least it seemed accepting. "Things fall on you. Responsibilities. Stuff you have to do. My name's Paul. Paul DeFiore."

He offered a hand with garnet-stained fingertips. She shook it and told him her name. Then she said, "Wine barrels?"

"Yeah. That's what I do. Make wine. Up in Los Olivos. Just bottled last year's vintage. Then it's time to scrub the barrels. The glitz, the glamour, right? Upside down, butt in the air, wrist-deep in crud. Looks funky, huh?"

She said nothing.

"Amazing pigments," he said. "Takes a week or two to wash away. Holds the aroma, too." He moved his fingers closer to his face, brought his long eyelashes together, and inhaled slowly. "Nebbiolo. My father planted it."

Involuntarily, he paused. He hadn't meant to talk about his father; somehow it just slipped out. Frank DeFiore had died seven years before in this same hospital. It was where father and son had had their final conversation, and the memory of those words and that parting made the building itself feel haunted. Paul didn't want to think about it, didn't want to jinx the present moment. Trying to rally, he forced a smile and went on. "Brought the vines from Italy. Sneaked them out, to tell the truth. Smells like cherry coke. Cherry coke and wild mushrooms."

Two things happened then, and it would be impossible to say which happened first. Darcy lifted her chin just slightly and leaned a little way into the neutral space between herself and the tall young man. He moved his hand a tiny distance in her direction. Like pairs of lips in an old movie, her face and his wine-stained fingers seemed to hang suspended for a time, hesitating, doubting. But in the next moment, there in the hospital waiting room, Darcy was leaning across, eyes closed, mind and senses riveted, breathing deeply of this stranger's wine-stained fingertips.

The improbable intimacy lasted several heartbeats. Then self-consciousness crept in, and Darcy backed away. Paul smiled at her; the smile, it seemed, was in equal measure shy and bold, and she couldn't help but smile back.

He asked her if she had time to grab a cup of coffee.

"So, who do you make wine for?" Darcy asked.

They were sitting in the hospital cafeteria. A less romantic venue could hardly be imagined. Ugly fluorescent lights flickered and hummed. Plastic trays scraped and clattered against formica tables.

Paul seemed slightly confused by the simple question. "For myself. Family winery. DeFiore Vineyards."

Flustered in turn, Darcy said, "I'm sorry. I guess I should know—"

He waved off the apology. "It's okay. We're small. Don't advertise. And I guess I'm pretty terrible at marketing. It's my absolute least favorite part of the job."

"What's your most favorite part?"

He sipped some coffee before he answered. "Everything else. The farming. The chemistry. The suspense leading up to harvest. But my absolute favorite part of all? The mystery. You do everything you can, use everything you've ever learned…but at the end of the day, the magic happens or it doesn't. You just can't know if you're going to end up with something really special."

Darcy found herself leaning forward. Corkscrews of russet hair tumbled down across her brow; she pushed them back though they quickly cascaded down again. "That's exactly how I feel about my own work. Cooking. Exactly the same thing."

"You're a chef?"

She raised a hand like a traffic cop. "Whoa. That word scares me. It's like when people call themselves artists. I don't like that. Call yourself by what you do. Painter, writer, whatever. The world will decide if you're an artist. Same with chef. I went to cooking school. I work in restaurants. I *cook*. Maybe someday I'll call myself a chef without blushing. But not yet. No way."

"But the mystery—"

"Right. Like some time you'll be working with ingredients you've used a thousand times before--tarragon, lemon zest, whatever— and something just happens. A dish goes to a different level. Do it consistently, you're a genius. For the rest of us, it's just a great surprise, a bonus…But I'll tell you one other thing I love about my work. You might get it or you might think it's weird. I love it that I give people pleasure without even meeting them. They're in the dining room, I'm in the kitchen. They don't know who made their food. I don't even want them to know. It's a gift and then it's over. I love that."

"I get it," Paul said. "But at the same time, with my wine, I sometimes think, wouldn't it be nice to be there when people are drinking it. Hear what they have to say, watch them enjoy it."

"I guess you're more sociable than I am."

"I don't know. You seem pretty sociable to me."

Darcy flushed at that. The flush brought out the green glints in her eyes and made her hair seem redder. "I'm usually not. I don't usually talk this much. The hospital, I guess I'm jumpy. Plus you're easy to talk to."

"So are you. Where do you cook?"

"Right now? Right now I'm at Santa Bistro."

Paul could not hold back a quick, soft laugh.

"What's funny?" she asked him.

"You say *right now* like it could change in twenty minutes."

"Well, it could. Couldn't it? I mean, things change. Most things don't last. Isn't that how it works?"

Paul studied the back of his spoon and considered. "I guess. Not for me, though. Not really. I live where I grew up. I do what I've always done. Better or worse, I seem to stick with things."

"I think that'd be nice," said Darcy. "Having something to stick with."

He shrugged. She looked down at her watch. She knew her father would still be in surgery, yet she felt a need to return to the waiting room. She felt a need, as well, to ease away from this easy-to-talk-to man who seemed to coax her into revelations without apparent effort or motive. "I should be getting back," she said.

He nodded and put their cups and saucers on the plastic tray. But they were still chatting as they left the cafeteria.

4.

Some time later, Hugh Barnett woke up in the recovery room. He was not in pain but he was very groggy. He blinked, turned his head, and fell back to sleep. This happened several times, and with each brief episode of consciousness he registered a little more of his surroundings.

The first thing he noticed was the lighting, which was a peculiar but soothing silvery green. Then he noticed the curtains on the windows. They billowed just slightly, though he could feel no breeze; they had a lovely shimmer, though he could see no light beyond the window frames. The room held half a dozen beds; his was the only one that was occupied. The place was marvelously silent; it lacked even the faint hums and creakings of merely quiet places. He took a breath of air that was scented with eucalyptus. He fell asleep again.

When he next awoke, a nurse was at his bedside. She was stately and crisp, with beautiful posture. Her uniform draped perfectly over broad shoulders and a comforting bosom. Her intricately folded hat rested lightly but solidly on her chestnut hair. She said, "How are you feeling, Mr. Barnett?"

"Not too bad. A little woozy, maybe."

"That's to be expected."

She reached down and took his wrist. She held her fingers against its underside though she had no watch to time the heartbeats.

Gesturing vaguely toward the empty beds on either side of him, he said, "Slow day, huh?"

"Ebbs and flows. Probably we'll fill up later."

"When can I get out of here?"

"It's a little soon to think about that." She smiled at him. It was a caring smile, confident and calm. "Let yourself relax a while. There's no reason to rush."

"Easy for you to say."

She sat down very lightly on the edge of the bed. This surprised him. Since when did nurses sit on beds? Even visitors weren't supposed to sit on beds. Wasn't that the rule? "Mr. Barnett, we have to talk."

"We are talking, right?"

"You're not exactly where you think you are."

In the mind of the groggy patient, confusion arrived before fear or panic. "I'm not in the recovery room?"

"You are in the recovery room. Just not the one you think."

He swallowed, glanced off toward the shimmering curtains.

"Mr. Barnett," the nurse went on, "when you were under anesthesia, did you have any dreams? Particularly vivid ones?"

He bit his lip, nestled deeper into his pillow, struggled to recall. "Yeah. Actually I did have one. I was floating. Couldn't say if I was going up, going down. Just floating. Now and then I'd sort of swim. I wasn't hot, wasn't cold, wasn't anything. Then I saw this kind of gleam. Hard to describe. Lots of colors all at once. Like neon, maybe, that wasn't in a tube. Just spread out everywhere. It sort of danced. You couldn't say if it was one inch or a thousand miles thick. I floated closer to it. Everything got blue. Then white. Too white. Blinding…That's all I remember."

The nurse said, "You were passing through the Membrane."

"Excuse me?"

"I'm sure you've heard stories, everybody has, of people surviving bad accidents or coming out of comas—they say they saw a distant bluish light? What they were seeing was the Membrane. The First Membrane. There are others. But anyway, they approached it and bounced off. You didn't bounce off. That's when the white light happened. You were passing through."

"Passing through," Barnett repeated numbly.

He stared up at the ceiling, trying to stay calm, struggling for clarity. He looked for evidence of his continued being, and had to admit that certain things were not quite right. He had no I.V. line in his hand; shouldn't it still be there? He reached up to touch his neck. There were no wounds, no bandages. How could that be? Almost accusingly, he said to the nurse, "But you took my pulse."

"Only to make sure you didn't have one. It's very awkward to have to send a person back."

The patient let his hands slap down against the sheet. He lay there silent for a while. If his situation was becoming clear, it yet remained unthinkable. A terrible, exhausting tension was building in his mind. How could a state of affairs be at the same moment completely undeniable and entirely inconceivable? Wrestling with this riddle made him frustrated; as the moments wore on without a resolution he found himself becoming very angry. "So you're telling me I'm fucking dead?"

Unflappably, the nurse said, "We prefer not to use that term. It has, let's say, negative connotations. We prefer to say you've been transmuted."

Barnett wasn't ready to buy it. "Transmuted my ass! Come on, it was a routine operation!"

"You were a little bit unlucky. Dr. Singh didn't have his best day. That's just how it goes."

"Great. He has a bad day and I'm transmuted. I'll sue the bastard! He's a quack."

"It's understandable that you're upset, that you're lashing out. But try to get over it. It doesn't help."

"Oh fine. Whatever. I'll just pretend it doesn't matter. La-di-da, I'm dead. But wait. I'm lying here. I have a body, I have eyes, we're talking—"

"You *seem* to have a body," she corrected. "It's a way of easing the transition, making things seem more familiar. And, in certain ways at least, things *are* familiar here. I think you'll be pleasantly surprised. But don't try to understand it all at once. It isn't possible."

He tried to speak again—to protest, to ask more questions— but realized all at once that he was far too tired. Like a distance runner at the finish line, his will collapsed abruptly; without gradation, he went from the blind assumption that he could run forever to the certainty that he could not take one more step. His arms were limp at his sides; his head lay on the pillow like a stone. A long moment passed. The curtains billowed softly. The greenish silver light bathed the room. Finally he managed to say, "My daughter."

The nurse said, "I understand. That's the part that hurts. Leaving people."

"She's waiting for me. At the hospital."

"Yes. She is. That's hard. I'm sorry for that, but it can't be any other way."

"I was hoping…" he began. "We were starting…" He couldn't find the words. His voice trailed off.

"Rest now," said the nurse. "It's really better if you rest."

5.

In the waiting room at Cottage Hospital, Darcy and Paul were chatting away. They talked about restaurants; they talked about books and movies. They talked about the miniature horses that were bred up in Santa Ynez, and the view from the top of Figueroa Mountain.

They were so involved in their conversation that they did not immediately notice when Dr. Sanjay Singh came into the room.

He was still in scrubs. His surgical mask was still tied around his neck; it hung down on his chest like a bib. He inquired at the volunteer desk and was directed to Darcy.

She looked up at the surgeon. His slight build and angular face accentuated the darkness and depth of his eyes. His lips were pulled into tight grayish furrows at the corners. He asked to speak with her in private. Her eyes brushed past Paul's as she rose from her chair, but in that moment she felt entirely alone, as if the fragile connection to this new friend had been suddenly wrenched beyond its limits.

Following the doctor out of the waiting area, she felt a sudden grab and a spreading burn in her stomach, as though she'd swallowed something much too hot. It was difficult to get her legs to move. Her knees would not bend, her ankles would not flex. She shuffled as if she were walking on ice.

Singh led the way toward a consultation room. The room was very spare. A desk; a few chairs; a box of Kleenex. The doctor did not sit down, but only leaned back against the desk, holding the lip of it with his long and well-trained fingers. He said, "Your father's surgery did not go well at all. I'm very sorry."

Darcy, suddenly, was having trouble with the meaning of even the simplest words. "Didn't go well?"

"He was much sicker than we realized. Even with all the diagnostics, there are things you can't know until you look inside. His blood vessels were very thin and brittle. They couldn't tolerate the clamps or the manipulation."

"So…"

"There was bleeding in the brain. It might have been possible to keep him alive, but he would have been severely compromised. That isn't what he wanted. We honored his directive. I'm sorry, but it's really better that way."

"He's gone?"

"He's gone. I'm sorry."

For a moment Darcy felt nothing. Grief required comprehension, and comprehension came on by grudging, difficult degrees. In the meantime there was only a supreme awkwardness in the consultation room. Singh wondered if he had said enough, if it would be decent now to slip away. He pushed the box of Kleenex toward Darcy. It was the cue that she should start to cry, but in fact she wasn't ready to. In her mind her father hadn't died yet. She needed at least a little time to retrace his passage, to imagine the calamity step by step.

Still, the surgeon was a busy man. He apologized yet again, and turned to go. Darcy's eyes followed him, and she saw Paul standing in the doorway.

He didn't speak. He stepped aside to let the doctor pass, then moved back to where he'd been. He didn't come into the room. He didn't know if he should. He and Darcy, after all, were little more than strangers who had met by merest chance on an awful day in a haunted place. The tiny increment of time they'd spent together was dwarfed and perhaps rendered totally unreal by the enormity of what had happened. What comfort could he possibly presume to offer? He stood there very still.

Darcy started to cry. At first there was no sound, just tears. She reached for the tissues and rattled the box with unsteady fingers. She looked up at Paul and said, "I wasn't even nice to him this morning."

"You were here."

She blew her nose. "Yeah. I was here."

They looked at each other but found nothing more to say. He wanted to open his arms to her, offer her a shoulder; it felt right to do that but he didn't think it was his place. Tentatively, he raised his hands; she leaned toward him as though to cry against his chest, but stopped a foot away.

After a moment she wiped her eyes, and said, "I don't even know what to do now. What needs doing when someone dies?"

6.

When Hugh Barnett woke up once again, the recovery room appeared quite different. Most of the beds were filled; now and then a gurney silently rolled by. Nurses scurried, each one with a maternal bosom and a perfect hat. Even with the quiet and the placid light, there was somehow a sense of bustle, of things that needed doing.

There was now an old man with a big and mobile face in the bed to Barnett's right. He had thin but rather frizzy white hair that rose in puffs on the sides of his head, leaving the top freckled and bald. His eyes were black and moist and lively, flashing under bristling brows and above purplish pads of skin. He had a large and friendly nose that seemed made less from cartilage than bread dough. His lips were full; the bottom one bowed out a bit.

The old man squinted over at Barnett, said a drowsy hello, then paused a moment to scan his memory. "Wait a second," he went on. "I think I know you. You're the weatherman, right? Channel six."

"Channel eight," Barnett corrected. Still, he was flattered to be recognized. "And I *was* the weatherman. They fired me three years ago. Soon as I hit sixty-five."

"Channel eight, right," said the man in the next bed. "I remember your face. Your name, I'm sorry, I can't. Names, since the tumor, give me all kinds of trouble."

Barnett told the man his name.

"Nice to meet you. My name's Manny. Manny Klein. They fired you? That's terrible."

"Way of the world. They called it a diversity move. Hired a Hispanic woman. She was very capable, very nice. But it wasn't about diversity. They wanted someone younger, period. So it goes."

Manny Klein gave his big head a sympathetic shake without quite lifting it from the pillow. His sparse hair picked up greenish tints from the odd lighting. "Must've been interesting being a weatherman."

Barnett came out with a small laugh. It was the first time he'd laughed since being transmuted. He was pleasantly surprised to discover that he could. "Interesting on the rare days we actually had weather. You know Santa Barbara. Morning fog. Light onshore breezes in the afternoon. Highs in the seventies, overnight low of fifty-five—"

"That's just like you said it on television!"

"Yeah, day after day, year after year. They could've just played reruns. And you? You work? Retired?"

Warming to the conversation, Manny Klein tried lifting up on an elbow. The effort seemed just a bit beyond his strength, and he called out to a passing nurse, "Hon, could you be an angel and bring me another pillow?"

When he'd been propped up he gave a dismissive wave, and said, "Me? I've been retired ten years now. I used to be a second fiddle."

"You mean, like, a middle manager? An assistant?"

"No. A second fiddle."

"Right. But second fiddle to what?"

"To the first fiddle. I played the violin. Thirty-seven years with the L.A. Phil. Sat in the middle of the section and played soft, so no one could tell if I was out of tune."

Beyond their beds, gurneys now and then criss-crossed. Over time it seemed less strange that their wheels made no sound, that the curtains billowed restfully although there was no breeze. Barnett said to his new friend, "I think you're being modest."

"No, I'm being honest. Look, you had to be pretty good to get into the orchestra. But there's good and then there's good. I was good enough to know how good I wasn't. Like Salieri. Remember Salieri from the movie?"

"*Amadeus*, right?"

"Right. Salieri was the only man in Europe who was a good enough musician to know that he was total crap compared to Mozart. He couldn't admit it to anyone. It would have wrecked his career. But he knew it. That was his torment."

"Was it yours?"

"Being second fiddle? Not at all. I had other torments, don't get me wrong. Who knows, maybe I just lacked ambition. But I was happy to sit there in the middle of the music and listen to the better players.

Besides, you can't have an orchestra where everyone's a first chair. That wouldn't be an orchestra. You know what it would be? Chaos. Really loud chaos. But enough about me. You, you look like a young man. You don't mind my asking, what brings you to the hospital?"

In that moment Barnett knew for sure what he had suspected all along—that Manny Klein was a newbie who hadn't yet been advised of his change of situation. It certainly wasn't the weatherman's place to clue him in. Casually, he said, "Getting some arteries unclogged. You?"

Klein pointed to his head. "Brain tumor. Been growing for years. Hardly noticed it at first. You know, I'm eighty-two, it's normal to slip a little, start forgetting names and so on. I wasn't worried till the sheet music started wobbling on the page. The staves got kind of wavy. Then I fell down once or twice. Okay, time to have it checked. They do tests and tell me *mazel tov*, you don't have cancer. Like cancer's the one and only thing that can go wrong in life. Your tumor's benign. I'm thinking *benign my eye! What's so benign about it?* I have a splitting headache, my foot is dragging on the ground. This is benign? Turns out the thing is like a wedge that's cracking my brain in half. Which is weird. I mean, think about a tumor—what do you picture? Either a little lump kind of thing or maybe something mushy, right? Mine's like a melon rind. Anyway, big time surgery. Fifty-fifty chance, they said. But here I am. My head doesn't hurt. That's got to be a good sign, right?"

Hugh Barnett was fumbling for something to say when a nurse glided silently between the beds. She gave the two men a breezy apology for disrupting their chat, then drew a curtain all around Manny Klein. Barnett, three feet away and separated only by a layer of the thinnest cloth, couldn't hear a word they said.

7.

It has sometimes been said that the loss of our parents is what finally turns us into grownups.

But Darcy Barnett, at least in the first flush of her bewilderment and grief, felt just the opposite. In the afternoon of the day her father died, she felt much more like a child than she had that same morning. For a few hours she sat in her apartment, sometimes crying, sometimes not, sipping wine, staring absently through the window, hoping for comfort or at least distraction in the familiar view outside.

Her place was three blocks from the beach in the blue-collar village of Carpinteria. It was a rather Spartan one bedroom, lightly furnished—an encampment from which a restless spirit could easily move on--in one of those classically shabby seaside complexes with carports on the ground floor and balconies with Astroturf carpet above. Still, she loved the place. Mostly young families lived there; the complex throbbed with life. On weekend mornings it was filled with the sound of plastic tricycle wheels grating against the concrete of the driveways. At quitting time on weekdays, a parade of pickup trucks came trundling home, and dozens of toddlers were hoisted in the air by strong-handed fathers in t-shirts. Darcy had always taken pleasure in the spectacle, much as she enjoyed the notion of other people savoring meals in restaurant dining rooms. She was soothed by the vitality around her; she shared in it without quite fully jumping in. Her neighbors looked out for her—a pretty single woman who got home late from work. She'd always felt not just safe in her apartment, but watched over, connected to others by thin but meaningful threads.

Today that sense of connection seemed to have vanished. Not only the vague but comforting connections with her neighbors, but all connections; even the connection between the person she'd been yesterday, when her father was alive, and the person she was now, an orphan. Continuity eluded her. She felt unmoored, dimly afraid, though of nothing in particular. She felt indistinct, as though she had no skin; she felt as if she did not know how to live.

From the outside, these feelings seemed to make no sense. She'd been on her own for nearly a decade; she'd proven again and again that she could take care of herself. She'd borne up under her mother's sudden death, nine years before. She'd zigzagged through school and chosen a profession. She'd always gotten jobs; she knew how to balance a checkbook. She entered rooms with poise and she was not afraid to talk to people.

Still, the loss of her second parent seemed somehow to negate her experience, to undermine her confidence. Just when it became complete and final, her independence suddenly seemed a bluff. What did she really know about life? What did she truly understand? Sipping chardonnay, looking through the slats of her blinds at yellow light and empty air, she felt that the answer was: almost nothing. Since leaving home, she'd been faking it and muddling through, pretending to a readiness and savvy she'd never quite believed in. Her father's death exposed the bluff.

But why? It was not as if her father had been a big part of her recent life. There'd been awkwardness between them, a jagged gap like a fissure in the ground. Now and then the jolt of an unkind word or a painful memory had made the fissure wider; mostly, though, it had spread by tiny increments, degrees too small to notice.

Even so, as long as her father was alive, there was the hope that the fissure could be mended, the distance could be bridged, and…what? That she might once again feel like a happy child in an intact family, secure in her father's nearness and his love? It was an absurd hope, impossible, ridiculous; the very thought of it embarrassed her. But in fact that hope was the crux of what she'd lost forever; the final flash and flameout of that hope was what was making her feel so much like a child. She was yearning to leapfrog back over the intervening years of adolescence and young womanhood, to dwell in the time before things had started going wrong, to revisit and erase the moments when damage had been done.

Well, that wasn't going to happen, and at some moment during that long afternoon she started to accept the fact. The acceptance did not take hold all at once, nor did it advance in steady fashion. Her mind plodded forward, her emotions slipped back like uphill footsteps on wet clay. Gradually, though, she was coming to inhabit the life she now had; in the space of a few hours she was growing up all over again. She pushed her thick, unruly hair back from her forehead and reminded herself that she was not, in fact, a kid. She found the phone book in a kitchen drawer and set about making the necessary arrangements.

8.

There was very little that needed doing around his mother's bedside, but Paul DeFiore wasn't good at sitting still, and he'd been sitting still for several hours, so now he fussed and fidgeted in the hospital room. He rearranged flowers that had been sent by friends and neighbors. He poured out water for his mother, bent her drinking straw just so.

Little by little, Rita DeFiore shrugged off the haze of anesthesia. Her gaze grew steadier, her voice got firmer. After a while she asked her son to find the hairbrush in her purse. A raven-haired beauty in her youth, she still retained a bit of vanity, mingled now with ironic decorum; at 74, she felt she shouldn't subject people to the sight of her unless she looked as good as she could manage. Not very skillfully, with the hand that was free of the intravenous line, she tried to smooth her rather brittle gray coif. When she was finished, her hair did not in truth look much different than it had before. But she felt far better about it.

She said to her son, "I'm really okay. You should go. I've wasted your whole day."

"No, you haven't."

She sniffed the air. "It smells like sick people."

"It's a hospital, Mom."

"It's where your father was. I don't like being here."

"Me neither. But it's where Dr. Sayre operates. Did you want a different surgeon?"

"You should go. You have a lot to do."

"Actually I don't," he lied. "The grapes will grow without me for a while. Trust me on this."

"Can I have a little water, please?"

He picked up the plastic cup with its bent paper straw. His mother tried to lift up from the pillow but found it very difficult. He supported her head with his other hand. He could feel the bones of her skull and the straining sinews of her neck. Her skin felt dry and very thin.

Settling herself with a wince she couldn't quite hide, she said, "The tomatoes are going to be really late this year."

"So let me put them in for you."

This was an ongoing routine with them, one that the old woman relished.

She said, "No. They're my tomatoes. I'll put them in. I never let your father do it. He did the grapes, I did tomatoes. One year I had pneumonia. You think the tomatoes didn't go in? You're not planting them either. They say six weeks rehab? Baloney. I'm doing it in three. Before I miss the season."

Her son went to the window and watched cars converge at a four-way stop. There was something genteel and dancelike in how they paused and then moved on.

Rita said, "You must be bored out of your mind."

"No. I had a nice conversation in the waiting room. Woman who really knows her food and wine. Time flew by."

"Single?"

"Mom, don't start."

"I'm not starting. I just asked if she's single."

"I don't know if she's single or if she isn't single."

And it was true. There were certain things about Darcy that Paul DeFiore had noticed. He'd noticed the candor, the curiosity, in her green-hazel yes. He'd noticed the set of her shoulders, a little tight maybe, but with a forward lean that struck him as courageous. He'd noticed the habit she had of brushing hair back from her forehead when a curl hung down and tickled; but never brushing it far enough so that it would not fall down again. But he hadn't been cruising the hospital for a romance. He was there for his mother, after all. Darcy had been there for her father, who had died, perhaps while they were talking about what wines to match with spicy foods. He hadn't noticed if she wore a ring. What was he going to do—ask her out while they both had parents on the operating table? Maybe, if the day had had a happier outcome, there might have been a chance…

"Who's she here for?" Rita pressed. "Mother? Father? Who?"

"Father," said Paul, and hoped he could manage to leave it at that. He'd felt the thinness of his mother's scalp when he'd helped her rise up from pillow. He'd felt how cautiously she'd settled back again. It seemed random and tentative and frightening that he should be here chatting with his mother while someone else that very day had lost a parent.

His mother shifted in bed, trying to get her new hip at a different angle. He could tell it hurt. "Should I ask them for a pain pill?"

"I don't want a pill. They make me stupid. I want to talk. I worry about you sometimes, Paulie. All you do is work."

"Not true."

She ignored the denial. "Ever since your father passed away. Ever since you came back from Europe. Work and worry, worry and work."

"Life intervenes, Mom. Dad was dying, I had to come home."

In Paul's case, life had intervened in a particularly abrupt and unlucky way. He'd been twenty-seven when his father, always vigorous and hard-driving, had suffered a coronary between two rows of his vineyard. An emergency bypass operation came too late; Frank DeFiore slipped into a coma and hung on, intermittently lucid, for five days. During that bizarre and exhausting interval, while his father drifted between life and death, Paul's own life was at first suspended, then changed in a way that was far more lasting.

Until that time, his life had seemed to be exactly where it should be. He'd gotten his degree in oenology, his passion field. He was in the midst of a time-honored apprenticeship in Europe, having worked a harvest in Tuscany, moving on the next year to France. In Burgundy, he'd been spending lots of days and nights with a fellow-winemaker named Clarisse. She was smart, ferociously opinionated, and very sexy, in a muddy-boots-and-dangling-cigarette kind of way. Paul thought they were in love—but whether it was with each other or simply with the adventure and promise of their separate lives, they were too young to know for sure.

"Okay, you had to come home," said his mother, cutting off his recollections. "Of course you did. For a while. But you could have gone back."

"No, I couldn't."

"Why not? We could have leased the vineyard, maybe even sold it."

"I just couldn't, okay?"

The truth was, he'd never told his mother, or anyone else, why he felt that he could not return to Europe. That was between his father and him. Deathbed chats, final wishes—if those things weren't secret and sacred, what was? Clarisse had understood without needing it explained; she herself was from a family that owned land and made wine and had passed the calling through the generations. Strangely, though, her serene acceptance of their parting had only made it harder for Paul. How could she be so calm about it? Did she have some wisdom, some certainty, that he lacked? Maybe this was just the deal: that family and legacy came first, and other dreams and possibilities fit in or did not.

His mother said, "I would have been all right. I really would have."

"Do we really need to talk about this now?"

She gave the smallest of shrugs against her pillow. "We're sitting in a hospital. What else is there to do? This girl from the waiting room. You'll see her again?"

Paul exhaled more emphatically than he'd meant to, then bit his lip to hold back any mention of what had happened to Darcy's father. "Mom," he fudged, "we were sitting just outside the operating room. People were getting transfusions, okay? Getting things cut out. It wasn't what you'd call romantic."

"Even better. If it's too romantic, roses, violins, how do you know it's the person and not the situation? Your father and I met on a pier."

"I know this story, Mom."

"I know you know it. But I still like to tell it. He was fishing. Not catching anything. I was taking a walk with my girlfriend Alice."

"A seagull stole Pop's bait," said Paul.

"Right. And he started yelling at the seagull, half in English, half Italian. Alice and I thought it was the funniest thing we'd ever heard. Then your father laughed too and we started talking. And I knew. Just like that I knew."

Rita smiled dreamily. She still loved that story. She could still see the dress she'd been wearing that day, blue background with white polka dots. She still remembered the red bandanna in the back pocket of her future husband's jeans.

"But Mom," her son went on, "that's way more romantic than a hospital."

"I guess. But my point is, where or when, you never know. That's all I'm saying. Where or when, it doesn't matter. Maybe I'll take that pain pill now."

9.

Hugh Barnett called out for a nurse.

He was feeling feverish. It was a different sort of fever from any he could remember. The heat of it did not seem centered in his skin, but much deeper within him, as though his bones had become hot coils, glowing red like the inside of a toaster. He didn't sweat; he didn't shiver; but the searing pulses throbbed through him like a false heartbeat.

Efficiently though without hurry, a nurse appeared at his bedside. He told her he was burning up.

"Yes," she said calmly, "you are. Your remains are being cremated."

"Cremated?"

"That was your instruction, I believe."

"Well, yeah, but—"

"But you thought it was just a word. We hear that a lot. It isn't just a word. It's an industrial process. But don't worry. It's not unusual for people to feel a kind of phantom pain. You're not yet entirely disconnected from your former body. Would you like a cool washcloth for your forehead?"

"Will it help?"

"Not at all. But some people take comfort from the familiarity of the gesture. You remember it from childhood, right? Your Mom bringing the washcloth soaked with alcohol or witch hazel in the middle of the night? But look, cremation's really not bad. It's not pleasant but it passes. Those who chose burial often experience a claustrophobic episode during the interment. That can linger. It isn't fun."

Barnett plucked at his sheets and endured another wave of broiling heat. He felt like the sun had lodged inside his ribcage.

"Think cool thoughts and ride it out," the nurse encouraged. "There is a payoff at the end."

"Payoff?"

"Once your ashes cool you can get up out of bed. You can move around."

"Move around where?"

The nurse didn't answer, but only reached up to make sure that her perfect hat was still perfectly in place before she walked away.

Barnett now found himself in a peculiar sort of garden. Not the Garden of Eden; nothing like that. No fruit trees, no animals from fables. This garden was completely austere, really just an infinite lawn with a very light contour to it here and there; it seemed like a setting for an opulent but tedious outdoor wedding, or a tea party with neither tea nor cakes nor thirst nor hunger. Iron tables and chairs were scattered about in no clear pattern; at some vague distance there were green- and white-striped tents. Barnett had the paradoxical impression that the garden was jam-packed and yet could never possibly be filled; he was dimly aware of presences all around him but they seemed to occupy no space.

He himself still had a body, or so it seemed to him. He could see his arms and legs; his feet connected with the lawn, albeit very lightly. He believed he still had his handsome face, though he hadn't seen it since his transmutation. He felt balloon-like, emptied out, as if his skin was wrapped around nothing but air. For some interval he wandered like a new arrival at a party, equally curious and uncomfortable, looking for a familiar face, a drink to occupy himself.

Then he saw his wife. His ex-wife. His dead wife.

It had been just over nine years since he'd seen her—a week or so before her fatal accident. The accident was no one's fault, just plain crummy luck. She'd been merging onto the northbound 101, driving the same route she'd driven thousands of times before, when an eighteen-wheeler blew a right front tire and came careening across her lane, pinching her between the trailer and the guard rail. She was killed instantly, and people, in their shock, said the usual self-comforting thing: at least she didn't suffer. But how did anybody know? What gave anyone the authority to say?

In any case, she came wafting across the boundless lawn, and in Hugh Barnett's mind there was no doubt whatsoever it was she, though her appearance was utterly remarkable. She seemed to be made of light, in tints of blue and pink and green; she looked like a hologram. Barnett felt that he was looking both at her and through her. Action lines spilled off her as she moved, as in a cartoon. Her hair—in life a rich russet, like her daughter's—was now represented by a somewhat fuzzy reddish nimbus; her bright black eyes were disks that shone in a face defined largely by negative space, except for her mouth, which, as ever, was wry and mobile.

Although he'd been feeling completely weightless, Barnett suddenly needed to sit down. He blundered toward a table. The table had a shade umbrella although there was neither sun nor shadow. He sat down in a metal chair, and all at once his wife was sitting opposite.

"Sheila!" he said. "What are you doing here?"

"Slumming, if you must know. Visiting from a way nicer place."

"Nicer place?"

"There's levels and levels, Hugh. I've moved on from this one. You'll eventually find out how it works. If you get that far. I'm not here to explain it."

He shot his ex a glance comprised of regret and remembered desire and a certain sheepishness about his past transgressions. He said, "God, it's really good to see you. But…you look so strange. It's you, and it isn't. Can I touch you?"

"Sure. Go ahead. Nothing will happen."

He could not resist saying, "Ah, just like old times."

As the words slipped out, a curl of light wrapped around his wrist and stopped the progress of his hand. Sheila said, "As I recall it, I cooled down when you did. But, of course, your energies were directed elsewhere."

Barnett looked down at his feet. "Come on, that was like a million years ago. Do we have to talk about it now?"

"Why not? Why not clear the air?"

"I just don't see—"

"Fact one about our marriage: You had affairs. Quite a few, I think. For a long time I suspected, but I hid it from myself. That was stupid. I admit it. I had my career, we had Darcy, I didn't want to turn things upside down. I should've kicked you out way before you left. Seems crazy now, but it was like I was too busy to make myself happy."

"You weren't happy? Not even at the start?"

"The funny part," she went on, "is that I always felt sort of sorry for you. Not for me. For you. I loved my work. You didn't love yours. I couldn't blame you. A weatherman in a place with no weather. But then I'd think, what, a hurricane or two to make you feel important, and suddenly you'd be a model husband and father? No, you'd be who you were. A pussy hound with capped teeth and a winningly boyish manner."

"I had to cap my teeth. They were crooked."

"That still leaves the pussy hound part."

Exasperated, Barnett said, "Sheila, what's the point of being dead if we're going to keep going over the same old crap as when we were alive?"

"The point is that now we can discuss it calmly."

The errant husband studied his former wife. It was true that she seemed perfectly serene; the light she was made of neither flashed nor pulsed nor dimmed. But he himself was getting very agitated. "Look, you're calm maybe—"

"Yes, I am. It's taken effort. There's a progression. In life, people go to great lengths not to tell the truth. Not to each other. Not to themselves. Especially themselves. Too dangerous, too upsetting. At your stage, the truth starts coming out. That's a good thing, but it hurts. Later, though—maybe—you get to a point where the truth no longer hurts. It's just there. It's neutral. If anything, the truth starts seeming kind of funny. Which is a big relief."

Barnett drummed weightless fingers on the metal table. "I'll take your word for it."

"But, listen," his ex went on, "I didn't come here to talk about us. We need to talk about Darcy."

A stab of worry knifed through Barnett. The emotion was painful but oddly reassuring. He hadn't known he was still capable of feeling such connection and concern. "Is she okay?"

"She's okay. Or okay as she can be. But she has some problems, Hugh. Problems you should have noticed but probably didn't. Our daughter takes after you in certain ways. She's charming without really seeming to try. She's magnetic, almost in spite of herself. And she's awful at relationships. She's allergic to good ones and addicted to bad ones."

Barnett was still close enough to his earthly existence that his first response was denial. "Come on, Sheila, don't be so dramatic. Allergic. Addicted. You've watched too many pop-psych shows. She just hasn't met the right guy yet."

"Don't be so sure. But that's not really the point. The point is that there's no such thing as the right guy for a woman who's sure from the start that things won't work out. Sure she'll be abandoned."

"Oh Christ, this again? Abandoned, like she was by her father? At the worst possible moment, just on the brink of womanhood? I know all this, Sheila. It was unfortunate. But—"

"Can we please move on? We're not talking about you. We're talking about our daughter. She goes to extremes. She meets a guy. Either she flees immediately or she falls in love way too fast. And you know what? Those are two sides of the same coin. Either way, what seems like a beginning is already an ending. Either it's over before it starts, or it has to burn out quickly, before she's put too much into it, before she has too much to lose."

"I really think you're exaggerating."

"I'm not. Trust me. I've been dead nine years. I've had a lot of time to watch. With Darcy there's no middle ground, no third option. All or nothing, and it ends up nothing. She's stuck in that pattern. Can't get out. And, excuse me, that's an addiction. Just like you with nicotine. A habit that becomes a prison. It tends to run in families."

"Oh, so I passed along the addict gene? That's my fault, too?"

"Let's stop talking about fault, okay? Let's try at least."

But Barnett was wallowing in guilt, almost enjoying it in some crazy way, and he wasn't about to be talked out of it so easily. "I have affairs, so our marriage turns lousy. I leave our lousy marriage, and my little girl feels abandoned. I pass along the addict gene, and my abandoned little girl is doomed to have the same disastrous date over and over again. It's on me. All of it. How can we not talk about fault?"

"You said it, not me. But around here we try not to be judgmental. Not small j, at least. Besides, I didn't come here to blame you."

"No? It sure sounds like you did."

"I came here to tell you you can help."

"Help? Help what?"

"Help your daughter. Help her get past this stuff."

"How can I help? I'm dead. I'm gone. It's way too late."

"It's not too late. Have you noticed people say that all the time? Living people, too? It becomes one more excuse."

"Sheila, I've flat-lined! I'm cremated!"

"Yes. And when your body was being burned, I'll bet you felt the heat."

"I did. Yeah."

"Which means you've still got some connection with your life. Which also means that, under certain circumstances, within certain limits, you're allowed to go back for awhile."

"Go back?"

"Just to visit. Tie up some loose ends."

"But how--?"

"That's all you need to know for now. You might have a chance to help your daughter. Think about it. What does she still need from you? Be ready."

Barnett started to speak again, but his dead wife was already dimming where she sat. The light she was made of didn't go out all at once but faded like dusk over water, her colors leaching toward a vacant lavender-gray, and the weatherman soon found himself alone at the table with the shade umbrella.

10.

Three days after her hip replacement, Rita DeFiore started rehab in the basement of the hospital.

Her son drove down to Santa Barbara to offer moral and, if necessary, physical support, but it turned out that not much help was needed. With a minimum of assistance, Rita could already get herself out of bed and into a wheelchair. From the wheelchair, craning her neck and flapping her arms somewhat in the manner of a baby bird, she was able to rise up onto a squeaky walker. The walker, in turn, quickly became the key to her mobility and freedom.

Squeaking along as she patrolled the hallways, she'd soon made friends with the day nurse and her fellow patients; she was already pressing her physical therapist for extra exercises, an accelerated regimen. Paul couldn't quite tell if his mother's ambitiousness was impressing the therapist or just driving her crazy. Rita needed to get out of the hospital and into an outpatient program closer to home. What was the soonest this could possibly happen? The garden couldn't wait much longer. The beds needed to be cleared of last year's roots and weeds. The tomatoes needed to be planted, then thinned, then staked. The marigolds needed to go in before the pests appeared. It was the busiest time of year. How long before she could lose the walker so that her hands were free to work? How long before she could kneel down on the ground?

After his whirlwind visit, Paul was very ready for a glass of wine.

He headed north again to Los Olivos, arriving just before six. The galleries and shops were closing down; the life-size plaster horse in front of the old tack and dry goods store was being wheeled in for the night. Soft light glinted off the tall flagpole that marked the center of the village. He headed to the Café.

To his relief, it wasn't very crowded. On summer weekends and at harvest time, the Café had in recent years become a tourist mecca; but here on a weeknight in early spring, it was still what it had started out to be—a locals' joint with a terrific wine list, where growers and reps and others from the trade could try each other's wares, look for their next job, and eat burgers at the bar.

Paul's friend, Josh Traber—a stalwart regular from the earliest days—was sitting at his usual place near a bend in the mahogany. Josh had shaggy brown hair that always seemed one week overdue for a trim. He was something of a superstar—winemaker and consultant to half a dozen pricey and prestigious labels—but you never would have known it from his wardrobe or his manner. He was an unassuming guy wearing a loose gray sweater and canvas sneakers with holes in them. His elbows were spread on the bar around three small glasses, each filled with a slightly different shade of gold. He spotted Paul and waved him over.

"Come check this out," he said. "Fascinating. Three chardonnays. Same vineyard—Bien Nacido. Same vintage—'07. Three different winemakers. These wines are nothing alike. It's all about what they do or don't do with the oak."

Paul managed a show of interest. Ordinarily, he would have been all over this kind of conversation. French oak, American oak. Large barrels, small barrels. Toasted, not toasted. At the moment he couldn't really think about it.

"This one," said Josh, "I wouldn't be surprised if it was stainless all the way. Lean, green apple. Could almost be a Macon or a Chablis. But *this* one—butter and papaya, it's oaked to the gills…You aren't listening, are you?"

"Actually," said Paul, "I sort of wasn't. Sorry."

He settled on a stool next to Josh. The bartender came over. Tonight it was Claudia. She'd been there for years. She knew the wines, the regulars, and how to keep a secret. She asked Paul what he'd like.

"Something red and not too heavy. Surprise me."

"So what's up?" asked Josh.

Paul didn't answer right away. He watched Claudia pour his wine. She poured with her back to him, from a bottle he couldn't see. It was a game they both enjoyed.

"Cheers," he said, when the glass was placed in front of him. Then, to Josh, he said, "I've really been wanting to talk to you. I had this crazy thing happen the other day. I met a really nice woman under sort of impossible circumstances, and I have no idea what to do."

Josh rubbed his hands together. "Oh boy, I love this kind of scenario. So tell me."

Paul paused to swirl and sip his wine; he put it down, considered, and tasted again. Then he called out to Claudia. "I think it's Tempranillo and I think it isn't local. It has the grip and that sort of dusty finish that usually means Spain. I'm guessing it's a young Rioja."

"You dog!" said Claudia. "Nailed everything except the age. Actually, it's an '03."

Paul shrugged. "Okay, makes sense. Hot, dry year. Slow to open up."

"Lucky guess," said Josh. "So anyway…"

"Anyway," said Paul, "I met this woman at the hospital." He told his friend about the waiting room, and the conversation over coffee—the ease with which it flowed, the mix of words and glances, the luxury of common ground. "And then it turned out that her father died."

"Died?"

"Died. On the table. Like twenty feet from where we were sitting. She got the news and must've been in shock. Maybe I was too. I mean, I've been there."

Josh kept silent and sipped wine.

"Anyway, I just stood in the doorway while the doctor talked to her. Felt totally helpless. Wanted to help. Wanted to hug her, drive her home, something, anything. But we were both, like, stunned, immobilized. Finally she walked away. And I haven't been able to get her off my mind."

Josh swirled wine, then held his glass up to the light to check its clarity.

"The thing is," Paul went on, "I can't even tell why I'm still thinking about her. I mean, is it even attraction or just sympathy?"

"Sympathy," said Josh, "you send a card. You don't agonize for days. You're attracted to her. Obviously."

"You say obviously. Nothing about this is obvious to me. I hardly know anything about her. For all I know, she could be married, living with someone."

"So find out. Call her up. A condolence call. Just to see how she's doing. What's wrong with that?"

A little sheepishly, Paul said, "Her number isn't listed."

"Aha!" said Josh. "So you've tried to call."

"I didn't say that. I tried to get her number. I hadn't decided if I would call or not."

"But why wouldn't--?"

"Maybe she wouldn't want to be reminded of that day, that room. Did you ever think of that?"

"Fair enough. On the other hand, going through something like that together, it could also be a bond. You said she's a chef?"

Paul gave a little laugh. "She doesn't like that word. Thinks it's pretentious. But yeah, she cooks."

"Where?"

"Place called Santa Bistro."

"Wow. Hot place. She must be good."

Paul shrugged.

"Why not call her there?"

Paul stared down at his Rioja. "I don't know. Calling someone you hardly know at work? Seems a little creepy. Stalkerish."

"You are one scrupulous son of a bitch."

"I just don't want to be a jerk about it."

"Sometimes a jerk is what you have to be," said Josh. "But let me offer another possible theory. Maybe you're just looking for excuses not to call."

"Oh, Christ," said Paul, "let's not start with the amateur therapy."

"Why not? Let's just think about it. How long have I known you? Six years?"

"Seven. You were just separating from your wife."

"You had to remind me?"

"It's just that you're such an expert on relationships."

"Other people's. I never said I was good at my own. But okay, seven. I don't know about every misadventure you've ever had, but I've seen you in a couple of situations. That woman from the Andrew Murray tasting room—"

"Jodi."

"Right, Jodi. Attractive, bright, perfectly nice. Lasted six months or so as I remember. What happened?"

"She bailed," said Paul. "Got frustrated that I didn't have enough time to give her. She was right. I don't blame her."

"Hold that thought," Josh said. "Then there was Alix, right, the one you met at the Foley crush party? Another six-month wonder, give or take. Why?"

"That time I pulled the plug," said Paul. "I felt too much pressure, too many demands."

"Voila," said Josh. "Déjà vu all over again. The only difference is who called it off. Bottom line, you just don't seem to have room in your life for a woman. Or at least you don't think you do."

"Well, I don't. With the vineyard, the winery, the business part, my Mom—"

"And yet," Josh interrupted, "now there's this new person, this elusive hospital woman, that you can't stop thinking about. Do you notice a certain contradiction there?"

"Thanks, Dr. Freud. Yes, I do."

Josh drained one of his chardonnays, then toyed with the base of the glass. "So here's what it comes down to. You need to see this woman again, if only to try and figure out what's what. But it can't be creepy and it can't be crass. She can't feel chased after while she's mourning, and you can't deal with pressure. Is that about right?"

Paul agreed that it was.

"Okay," said Josh, "let's have more wine. We'll figure something out."

11.

After his former wife had dimmed and vanished, Hugh Barnett spent an interval of time wandering at loose ends across the boundless lawn with its scattering of striped tents and shade umbrellas. He vaguely sensed a multitude of beings whom he could not see or hear; they seemed to slip past like a giant school of silver fish, veering now in complex parallels, darting away in a silent horde, all around him yet never colliding. Then at last, amid the flow of slipping spirits, he saw someone—a person with a face and at least the outline of a body. Someone he could talk to. He was so happy and relieved that he fairly sang out, "Manny!"

"Hey, weatherman," said his acquaintance from the recovery room. "Sorry, tell me your name again?"

Barnett refreshed his memory and asked him how he was.

"Better now. But, wow, I had a tough time in there."

"Tough how?"

"Panic attack," said Manny. "I saw this shrinking little crack of light, then everything went black. I couldn't draw a breath. I couldn't move my arms. I felt like damp and dirty roots were scratching at me. Everything was freezing cold and musty."

"You asked to be buried, right?"

"Yeah. It's a Jewish rule. They have to put you in the ground. Don't know why they started that. Probably you end up fertilizer. Lousy soil in the Holy Land."

"I was cremated," said Barnett. "That was no picnic either."

For some reason Manny Klein started laughing. His moist black eyes crinkled up, his fluffy white hair shook just slightly.

"What's so funny?"

"We are. Old men are. First we spend years talking about our aches and pains and prostate glands and how much we have to pee, now we're still talking about the *tsuris* with our dead bodies. What's next? Oy, I got such a cramp in my wings! Anyway, what's to do around here?"

"Do? I'm not sure *do* is exactly the right word. I did have a visit with my wife."

"You got to see your wife?" said Manny Klein. "That's wonderful."

Barnett said nothing.

"It wasn't wonderful?"

Barnett looked down and toed the turf. "We had a difficult marriage. Ended in divorce. My fault mostly. I played around."

"Why'd you do that?"

The simple question was entirely neutral, and Barnett found its candor utterly disarming. He gave the quick nervous laugh that people often feature when a shred of their defense is being stripped away.

"I did it…" he said. "Why *did* I do it? It's crazy, but while I was doing it I didn't really think about why. I did it because I did it. But I guess it was because something was missing. Not in Sheila. Not in the marriage, exactly. In me."

"If it was missing in you," asked Manny, "what made you think you'd find it somewhere else?"

A fair question, but Barnett let it pass. "I never settled on exactly who I was," he said. "Part of it was my profession. Was I just the talking head who stood there with his finger on the radar map? Was this my life? I'd wanted to be an actor. I took a lot of classes. Scene reading. Improv. And the plain truth is that I wasn't very good. No, let me revise that. I was awful. I was all outside, no inside. Perfect for TV, right? But on stage I was a bad bluffer and I knew it."

Manny scratched his flubbery and friendly nose. "Bear with me a minute. I'm not sure I follow you. You screwed up your marriage because you were a lousy actor?"

"It wasn't only that. I'll tell you a secret. Deep down, I always knew my wife was smarter than I was. Plus, she loved her work. She produced the five o'clock news show. You know what that means? She *decided* what the news was. Think about that. The privilege, the responsibility. She decided what should be on people's minds. Plus she wrote most of the stories, made the anchors sound clever or sensitive or whatever. Me, what did I get to decide? Which way the wind was blowing?"

Manny rubbed the corners of his wide mouth. "So you were a bad actor, and your wife was smart, and *this* was why you had affairs?"

"Yes. No. Wait." Barnett made vague circles with his upturned hands. "This is crazy. I had reasons. I know I had reasons. People do things for reasons, right? But when I try to put it into words…Look, I'm getting all confused. Can we talk about something else? What about you?"

"What?"

"Your wife. Your marriage. Was it good, bad? Were you happy, unhappy?"

"None of the above," said Manny. "I never married."

"How come?"

"I don't think I'm going to tell you."

"Gay?"

"Not gay. Just because I play the violin you think I'm gay?"

"I didn't say I think you're gay. I just asked why you never married."

"And I said I'm not going to tell you."

"Why not?"

"Because you'll laugh."

"I won't laugh. Why would I laugh?"

"Why? Because it's very romantic, and when an old man tells a love story, let's face it, it's ridiculous."

"I won't laugh," said Barnett. "I promise."

Manny looked off toward one of the distant green-striped tents. "You think we could get a cup of tea or something?"

"I don't think there is any. I've never seen anybody having tea."

"Mind if we check at least?"

With modest strides that somehow gobbled up large distances, they quickly came to a green-striped tent. Moving the flap aside, they found a teapot and two cups laid out on a table covered with a clean white cloth.

"Amazing," said Barnett.

"Ask and ye shall be given," said Manny. Sitting down, he added, "Some cookies would be nice."

He looked upward as if expecting a plate of petit fours to descend from the ceiling of the tent. Nothing happened. "Okay," he said, "I won't push it."

Sipping tea, Barnett said, "You were about to tell me why you never married."

Manny Klein fingered his teacup, let it rattle a bit against the saucer. Then he said, "Okay. It's really pretty simple. I met the love of my life a little too early. We were too young to understand how good we had it, how rare it was. We let it get away. And I never felt the same again. There. That's it. That's the short version."

"What's the long version?" Barnett asked.

12.

Darcy had taken a few days off from work, and when she returned to Santa Bistro, in time for lunch prep on a weekday, she was met by a cluster of small kindnesses.

Her cooking smock, with her name embroidered on the pocket, had been crisply pressed and hung on a hook like a welcome sign. Neatly placed beneath it, the clogs she wore while working the line had been buffed clean of their assorted drips and spatters. The head chef, her pal Nadine, presented her with a condolence card signed by the entire staff; the pastry chef, Miguel, handed her a wonderful tart made from marzipan and pears.

She was grateful for the gestures, the more so because she truly had not expected them. The restaurant business was funny that way. If the tight quarters and time pressure of the kitchen enforced a certain type of intimacy, the nature of the work and of the people who tended to choose it also imposed a kind of distance. It was, for the most part, a transient industry, an industry of wanderers and exiles, of people who didn't necessarily love to go home. To work in restaurants was to live life upside down, working hard while others took their leisure, sleeping while other people made their livings. Within this contrarian and isolating schedule, people came and went. Today's colleague was tomorrow's competitor; friendships were intense but tentative, worn down sometimes by series of small frictions, or exploded in one hot burst of temper. Chefs traveled with their own sets of knives, and this was as telling a tradition as that of samurai with their swords. At the end of the day, one's own tools and skills and passion were the only things that could consistently be counted on.

All of this suited Darcy's temperament—people, after all, did not choose their professions by accident. Still, she was both touched and surprised by her co-workers' show of concern. Her manner, she felt, did not invite that sort of thing. Not that she was unfriendly; not at all. In the kitchen she was animated, chatty, sometimes downright goofy at the end of a manic and exhausting shift. But, those moments aside, she was essentially reserved; self-contained might be a better way to put it. Physically strong, crisp and decisive in her gestures, she just didn't seem to need much from anyone. This stoic attitude had sometimes discouraged others from offering kindness; and it had usually made it difficult for Darcy to accept kindness, even when the kindness had been freely given.

Today it all felt slightly different. She let the gestures of concern wash over her and through her. She was touched and let it show. What had changed? Maybe this new openness was just a temporary side-effect of grief, a symptom of emotions rubbed raw. But perhaps it was the beginning of a more durable development; maybe the loss of her second parent was nudging her toward full adulthood, after all. Alone now, accountable only to herself, she somehow felt that she had less to hide, less to protect herself against. Somehow, these last few days of mourning, of reconciling, had made her feel more assured, more solid in the middle; the feeling, in turn, made it seem less scary to show some softness at the edges.

The tempo of restaurant work, however, allowed for only fleeting moments of introspection, and Darcy soon threw herself into the tasks before her; their familiarity was the biggest comfort of all. She lifted the lid of the giant stockpot and breathed deeply of the restorative vapor—carrots, onions, and the intoxicating richness of melting marrow. On a chrome counter away from the heat and the steam, she found a basket of chanterelles brought in earlier that morning—a treasure discovered by one of the local mushroom hunters who secretly patrolled the hidden creases in the hills above town. There were shallots to chop, scallions to dice, red and yellow peppers to turn into confetti. She reached for her knives, and found that they had all been sharpened in her absence. People, she reminded herself, could be as nice as she would let them be.

She was peeling and deveining prawns when Nadine came over to ask how she was doing. Nadine had short, spiky blond hair and a small flower tattoo on the left side of her neck. She was brilliant in the kitchen, drank bourbon after work, and had become a trusted friend.

"Fine," said Darcy. "I really think I'm fine."

"I'm glad you're back. But see how it feels. If you need more time, we'll manage."

"Thanks. But I think I'm better off working. How long can you stare out the window?"

Nadine patted her shoulder. "See the chanterelles? We're doing a risotto with a duck reduction, maybe a few toasted hazelnuts. Oh, and one other thing. We're tasting some wines tomorrow. Four o'clock. You're invited."

Darcy kept on peeling prawns, bending them backwards to free up the little armor plates.

"Small producer called DeFiore. Ever hear of them?" Nadine was not a coy individual, but there was something coy in how she said this.

"Maybe. I think so."

"The winemaker himself called up. Hoping to get on our list."

Darcy said nothing, just slit another prawn and carefully scraped away its gut.

Nadine said, "I sort of have the impression he's doing this for you."

"Oh?"

"Want to know the first clue? He very casually asked if you'd be working that day. Is there something you'd like to tell me?"

Darcy shrugged and put down her knife. She gathered up the prawns and put them in a bowl, then drizzled them with olive oil and spangled them with pepper. Finally she said, "We met at the hospital. We were talking when I got the news. Other than that, it's all a bit of a blur."

In this she was not being completely honest. Certain things about Paul DeFiore she remembered quite clearly. His wine-stained fingertips. The surprising mix of light blue eyes and jet black hair. Most vividly of all, she remembered him standing in the doorway of the consultation room. Why had he followed her there? They were strangers; he didn't have to do that, didn't have to share her grief. He'd looked so sad for her. He'd offered comfort. Offered without insisting. She might have cried against his chest. Might have, but couldn't.

"I don't think I'll go," said Darcy.

Until the words were out, she had no idea she would say them, and even afterward she wasn't at all sure why she did. Maybe it was just that her emotions were still too bruised. Or maybe it was an old reflex to fend off anything that felt too right, anything it would hurt to want and lose.

Nadine shrugged. "Your call."

Darcy said nothing and her friend pushed it a bit. "He sounded like a really nice guy," she went on. "But hey, what do I know, I've been a dyke since boarding school."

"Lucky you," said Darcy. "Me, I seem to be stuck with liking men. Just usually not the right ones."

"If it's any consolation, there's plenty of wrong women too."

"I'll take your word for it."

Trying a different tack, Nadine said, "Look, even if the guy turns out to be a dork, the wines might be good."

Darcy said nothing, just picked up a lemon and started zesting it; the fragrant curls of yellow peel wound down into the bowl of prawns.

Nadine patted her shoulder once again. "Okay. No pressure. Just thought you might enjoy the company. Why don't you decide tomorrow?"

13.

In the green-and white-striped tent, Manny Klein was pouring out more tea and gingerly easing in to the love story that was the fondest souvenir from his recently ended life. Reluctant at first, afraid of sounding ludicrous—an old man with slack skin and wispy white hair channeling a young man's hopes and ardor—he only gradually caught fire with his tale but then told it with relish.

"We were twenty-two," he said. "So that was, what, sixty years ago. Nineteen-fifty. We were second-year students at the conservatory. Eastman, in Rochester, New York. Great school. Nice town, too, if you don't mind freezing your ass off.

"I met Emma in a chamber music class. Emma Winthrop. I can still remember what she was wearing the first time I saw her. Which is crazy, right? You get to a point where you can't remember where you put the car keys two minutes ago, but something from a previous century stays right before your eyes. It was one of those dresses that the women all wore back then—little round collar, buttons down the front, then a wide skirt that came down just below the knees. It had an off-white background with a green pattern that made me think of Spearmint Leaves, that old jelly candy you ate in the movies. Her hair—there was something playful about her hair. It was dark brown, wavy, and it came exactly halfway down her ears. It bounced when she played. She had dark eyes that I guess you'd call almond-shaped. Sometimes, when she was concentrating really hard, the tip of her tongue moved to the corner of her mouth. Always the left side. Never the right.

"She was a cellist. Let me tell you something. There's a lot of bullshit cello-playing in the world. It's a hard instrument. Lots of space between notes, very easy to get off-pitch. Tone's a problem, too. If you can't find the warmth, it just sounds like bees buzzing in a jar. Some people get so hung up on technique, they forget it's supposed to be music. Other people seem to think that, if you give it enough feeling, it'll cover up the sloppy playing, the sliding all over the place. Emma wasn't like that. She was a beautiful player.

"We started playing quartets together. I looked forward to those rehearsals more than anything. Emma had this thing she did, it drove me crazy. Just a certain way she gathered up her skirt so she could settle the cello between her knees. The way she did it wasn't flirty, wasn't bashful, just unself-conscious and graceful. Just something you did if you were a woman cellist. Which was another funny thing. She was the woman, but played the lower-pitched instrument. I was the man, but played the higher one. It fit our personalities. She was mellow, cozy, dignified. I was a little jumpy, outgoing, maybe a little shrill sometimes.

"You have to understand that playing string quartets is very intimate, very sexy. You need to pay attention to each other in a way that people hardly ever do. You need to answer every tiny lift of an eyebrow, every slight tilt of a shoulder. It's a dance. When she leans, you lean. When the music shrinks down, you both shrink down together, like you were squeezing side by side through a low and narrow doorway. When the music swells, it's like you're both inflated, floating like balloons in a parade, your whole expression changes, shoulders open up, you rock from the waist…It's fantastic. By the second semester, we were spending lots of time together."

"You were lovers?" asked Barnett.

Manny took a small sip of his tepid tea. "Lovers," he said. "People use that term so easily. Like it's no big deal. Eventually, yeah, we were lovers. Don't laugh—both virgins up till then. About as nervous and clumsy as you'd expect. Still, it was wonderful, amazing.

"It was also terrifying. This is what people don't understand. It was such a different time. People slept together; sure they did. You think sex was invented at Woodstock? But there were consequences. Birth control was primitive. And if you slipped up, then what? We were supposed to have careers. Our families had sacrificed, buying instruments, paying for lessons, sending us to school. Making love put all of that at risk. But not making love now seemed impossible. It was a tightrope walk. Exciting, sure. But also a strain. I think it wore us down."

"So you broke up?" asked Barnett.

"Not right away, no. We lasted just over a year. But I'll tell you something I didn't realize at the time. In some crazy way, the breakup started when we went to bed. Because the stakes just got too high. We loved each other. We tried to tell ourselves that loving each other was just as important as our futures in music. Unfortunately, that was bullshit. Here's a basic fact: No two things are ever equally important. Never. One is more. One is less. People bend over backwards to deny it, but that's just how it is. At some point you have to choose.

"The crunch came in our third year at school. The orchestra auditions. Emma was offered a chair in Philadelphia. The Philadelphia under Ormandy! Greatest string section in the world. Of course she had to take it. Me, I got L.A. Funny thing—L.A. these days is as good as any of the eastern outfits. Back then it really wasn't. So I was second fiddle in a second-tier orchestra. Story of my life."

"And the relationship?" asked Hugh Barnett. "It ended?"

"Slowly. Painfully. You know how it is with first love. Or, who knows, maybe you don't. People don't let go all at once. It hurts too much. So you string yourself along, imagining the love affair is still alive. But what was there to keep it going? Some long distance phone calls that we couldn't really afford? The possibility of seeing each other once or twice a year, a couple of weeks in summer? It wasn't enough. Not even close. Finally we called it off. I think we both knew we had to, but it was Emma who really took the lead. Which made sense. She was always the more realistic of the two of us. Women usually are."

"And when it was over?" said Barnett.

"When it was over—what?" said Manny. "Time passed. Life went on. For a while I was devastated, miserable. Let's face it, young people are all drama queens. Everything's a tragedy. Like every other young man with a broken heart, I was sure that no one had ever suffered like I was suffering, no one had ever dealt with such a loss. I sat in my apartment, drank sherry, and played the saddest music I could think of.

"But here's the thing. Even when I was most down in the dumps, totally wallowing, I secretly believed that everything would turn out fine. Not tomorrow. Not next week. But in the long run, absolutely. I'd meet another woman as wonderful as Emma. Who knew—maybe even more wonderful. We'd fall in love, we'd make love—it could be better than anything I'd ever known.

"Why did I believe that? One reason. I was young. I had time. Everything was stretching out in front of me. The world was full. How could something happen only once? Things happened again and again. What I'd felt with Emma—I was sure it could happen again. Except it didn't."

"You never fell in love again?"

"Not like that first time. Look, don't get me wrong. I haven't lived as a monk. I've had some nice relationships with a few terrific ladies. I've enjoyed companionship, conversation. Sex too, okay? At moments I've even felt pretty damn romantic. But it's also true to say that I've been missing Emma for almost sixty years."

Barnett looked away a moment, hid behind his teacup to give his friend some privacy. Then he said, "So what became of her? Did you stay in touch?"

"For awhile. Then it got sort of awkward. She married a pianist. Fine musician. They even did some recording together. She had two children. Stayed with the orchestra her whole career. She died around nine years ago. Lymphoma. I heard from an old classmate at Eastman."

"You never saw her?"

"Not since, what, 1954. I never heard she was sick, only that she'd died. If I'd heard in time, would I have gone to see her? I don't know. I don't know if I would have had the nerve. Anyway, it didn't happen."

He reached for the teapot. It was an old-fashioned shape, with a graceful curving spout such as genies emerged from in old picture books. He starting pouring tea, then stopped. "Hugh," he said, "can I ask you an odd sort of question?"

Barnett nodded.

"You can see me, right? I mean, I look more or less like a regular living person to you?"

"More or less. Yeah."

"Good. And I can see you. But no one else. Not so far at least. It's very strange. I have this sense of people all around, packed in like commuters getting on a train in Tokyo. But I don't feel crowded and I don't feel bodies and I don't see faces."

"Same for me. I didn't want to come right out and say it."

Manny rubbed his broad soft mouth. "But I see you and you see me, and we're sitting here together drinking tea and swapping stories. I wonder why that is?"

14.

Young love. Missed opportunity. Those were the subjects on Hugh Barnett's mind as he emerged from the tent and resumed his wandering across the boundless lawn. He was only half-surprised when he once again saw his dead wife suddenly loom up before him.

As before, she seemed to be made entirely of light, yet her contours, to her former husband, now seemed more substantial. She hadn't changed; rather, it was as if, in some unearthly way, his vision had adjusted or phased into some different sense for which there was no name among the living, so that the previously ethereal now seemed made of solid stuff. Before, Sheila's eyes had appeared to him as shiny, reflective, doll-like disks; now he saw farther into them, into the changeable depth where humanness resides. Her shoulders, previously nothing more than sweeps of light, now suggested warmth and texture; with a pang, he recalled when her shoulders had been made of flesh, and he'd laid his head against them in the mornings, before his gallivanting had spoiled things.

She said, "Hello, Hugh. Feeling brave today?"

"Brave?" He'd never considered himself especially brave; why should he start now?

"It's an important day for Darcy," Sheila said. "Maybe a really crucial day. Maybe you can help."

"Help with what?"

"An opportunity."

Barnett gestured vaguely back toward the tent where he'd recently been drinking tea. "I was just talking with a guy who missed his opportunity. Regretted it for sixty years."

"Funny how things happen around here, isn't it? Almost as if there was a plan. Come with me. I want to show you something."

Without another word, Sheila scudded off. She seemed to be traveling at great speed, yet Barnett had no trouble keeping up. He felt that he was taking ordinary footsteps but there was no relation between the length of his stride and the distance that he covered. At some point they came to a kind of edge, the merest suggestion of a boundary. It was marked only by a low white fence such as one might put around a flower bed.

In front of the fence was a viewing device just like the ones you see at certain vista points or oceanfront esplanades. Mounted on a sturdy green base, it was shaped rather like a smiley-face made of hammered aluminum: the lenses were the eyes, the focus knob was the nose, and the coin return slot was the mouth.

Barnett looked dubiously at the gizmo. "Those things never work," he said. "You put the money in, and either the shutter doesn't open, or just when you find what you want to look at, it shuts again. They're a rip-off."

Patiently, his wife said, "Here they work. And you don't even need quarters. Come on, take a look."

The weatherman stepped forward and peered through the viewer. To his surprise, he saw—in nearly perfect focus, though with a bit of fade and glare along the edges—a modest stucco house set on a hillside; its roof was made of terracotta tiles. Behind the house was a garden that seemed unworked so far this spring; in dry, raised beds, leaning stakes were wrapped in the tatters of last year's tomato plants. Beyond the garden, moving upslope, there was a barn-like structure, made of stone and supported by sweeps of piled earth; then a vineyard stretched away. The soil between the rows of vines was very red; the new growth at the tips of the plants was an explosive yellow green.

"Looks like Tuscany," said Hugh.

"You're close. It's California. About twenty miles from where we used to live."

"I thought it looked familiar."

"A little side road in Ballard Canyon. Just up from Los Olivos."

"So why am I looking--?"

"Look again," she said.

Barnett returned to the viewer and this time he saw the inside of the house. It was simple but cozy. The walls were white plaster that still showed trowel marks. The windows were framed in dark wood;

above a stone fireplace there was a mantel covered in a tangle of family photos.

Standing at the kitchen stove, a tall young man was flipping fried eggs in a pan—flipping them as gently as he could so as not to break the yolks.

Sitting at the kitchen table, an aluminum walker at her side, a handsome old woman with silver hair was waiting for her breakfast.

Barnett retreated from the viewer. "Okay, some guy is making eggs."

His wife said, "Doesn't he seem like a nice young man?"

"How should I know?"

"See how careful he is with the yolks? He's trying really hard to have them come out just the way his mother likes them."

"Look, Hitler might've flipped eggs for his mother. I don't see—"

"He's a nice young man," said Sheila with finality. "And I think he may be Darcy's last best chance at happiness."

This was said with such simplicity and conviction that it briefly silenced Hugh but also made him skeptical. "Since when do you go in for such dramatic pronouncements?"

Calmly, her light neither flashing nor dimming, Sheila said, "Since I cleared the Second Membrane. Since I started seeing things more clearly."

"Second Membrane?"

"We'll get to that. But for now we're talking about Darcy and this young man. His name is Paul DeFiore. They met at the hospital."

"At the hospital?"

"In the waiting room outside of surgery."

"Oh, nice. I'm getting my neck cut open and she's making whoopee."

"She wasn't making whoopee. Neither was he. That's the whole point. Don't you see? He was there for his mother. Darcy—don't ask me why—was there for you. It was an emotional day. Their hearts were full. But not for romance. Romance was the last thing on their minds. That's what made it special."

"Special. My brain is bleeding and for her it's special."

"Hugh, will you please put your own little problem aside and try to understand? Darcy doesn't do well with a direct approach. That's a big part of her problem. A guy shows interest, or she feels a strong attraction, and right away the anxiety kicks in. She needs something that just sort of sneaks up on her. Takes her by surprise, gets her when her resistance is down. Like in a hospital, okay? That's what made this different. That's why I think it could work."

Absently, Barnett toed the turf of the gigantic lawn. He went once again to the viewer. The old lady was happily mopping egg yolk with a piece of toast. The young man was drinking coffee from a big brown mug.

"This guy—how old is he?"

"Thirty-four."

"Ever been married?"

"No."

"Thirty-four. Never been married. Still lives with his mother. That worry you at all?"

"He doesn't live with his mother. He lives with his wine."

"Excuse me?"

"That stone building. It's the winery. He built himself a loft apartment there. He's obsessed with his wine, obsessed with his work. That's going to be one of the big challenges in getting them together."

A little slow on the uptake, Barnett said, "Getting them together?"

Swallowing back exasperation, Sheila said, "What else do you think this is about? I'm not doing a goddamn travelogue. This is where you can help."

"I still don't see--"

"He's going to Darcy's restaurant today. Supposedly, it's to sell them wine. The real reason is he wants to see her again. But he doesn't want to pressure her at all. I think that's extremely considerate of him."

Barnett, a chronic pursuer of women, thought it over. "Pretty suave, too."

"Figures you'd see it that way. But whichever it is, she doesn't want to be there."

"Doesn't want to be there? Why not?"

"Think about it, Hugh. Use your limited imagination."

He chewed his lip. "I guess because of how they met. She doesn't want to be reminded."

"That's part of it. You're dying definitely put a crimp in things."

"Oh, so that's my fault too? Well, let me tell you something. It's not my fault I died. It's Singh's fault. That fraud. That butcher."

"Let it go about Singh, okay? Besides, your dying is only part of the reason. She doesn't want to go because she really liked the guy, and if she sees him again, she's afraid she'll like him more."

"This is a reason not to go?"

"For Darcy? Absolutely."

"So what am I supposed to do?"

"You're supposed to help her change her mind."

"Change her mind?"

Sheila said, "You can go to her. I think this is the time."

Barnett suddenly felt overwhelmed and dizzy. His knees went weak and he sat down on the lawn. The turf was neither cool nor warm beneath him. Sitting did not do much to quell the dizziness. Finally, he said, "I can talk to her?"

"Talk? Not exactly. You won't have a body down there. You won't have a voice. Still, you do have a bag of tricks at your disposal. You can show up in dreams. You can steer thoughts, ease fears, call up memories. You'll figure it out."

Still sitting, still feeling overwhelmed, Barnett said, "I just don't see—"

"Here's what you have to remember," said his former wife. "Here's what you have to believe: You're dead, but then again you're not. You're still in other people's lives. For a few people at least, you count. That gives you power. You can help people heal, nudge them toward happiness. Is that a privilege, or what? So, do you want to try it? Yes or no."

Groping toward conviction, Barnett said, "Well…of course I do."

"Not so fast. Full disclosure. It's grueling and dangerous. You have to pass back and forth through the Membrane. Plus, there's no guarantee that you'll be able to make things better. You might even make them worse. And there's a chance you might get trapped."

"Trapped?"

"Stuck in the middle between here and there. A.k.a, obliterated. It's a risk. You don't have to do it. You really don't. If you want to stay right here, no one's going to blame you."

"Not even you?"

"Not even me."

Barnett wavered. He remembered his transmutation only hazily, but well enough to recognize that traveling between worlds was no small matter—the shredding of time, the blasts of light, the rending and reassembly of his very being. But what frightened him more than any of that was something else his wife had said: that by showing up he could actually make things worse for Darcy. Alive, he'd failed as a husband, failed as a father. Dead, the guilt remained but at least the failing was over. Or was it? What paralyzed him for the moment was the prospect of failing yet again.

Then something else occurred to him. It was a grand and noble thought, a notion that briefly filled him with courage. He said, "This is the way to redemption, isn't it?"

To his surprise, his dead wife, traced out in her intersecting strands of light, laughed at him. "Piece of advice, Hugh? Lose the big words. Redemption. Salvation. Paradise. They're beautiful words, but the problem is that no one has a clue what they really mean. So stick to basics. You have a chance to make things better for your daughter. Isn't that enough?"

15.

As she did nearly every morning, Darcy was running on Carpinteria Beach.

It was a beautiful though undramatic beach—broad, flat, benign—much nicer, all in all, than the ocean it fronted. The ocean in that part of the world was a giant tease, colder than it looked, fickle in its promise of waves, a murky gray-green in color. Surfers loved it with a stubborn love; certain hearty swimmers—Darcy among them when she felt the need of something bracing enough to overwhelm thought and put all moods on hold—would brave the chilly surge beyond the surf zone, emerging with skin that tingled head to toe and goose bumps that lasted half an hour. For most people, though, the attraction of the beach was the sand and not the water.

The sand was different at every hour. Close to dawn, when the ambitious nine-to-fivers did their jogging, the sand was damp and heavy with fog; it flew from people's running shoes in little clumps like the topping on a coffee cake. But Darcy, living as she did on a restaurant schedule, ran much later in the morning. By the time she'd jogged the three blocks from her apartment and skipped down the funky wooden staircase from the street, the sun had generally broken through, and the sand, now a paler shade of gold, had dried to the consistency of cornmeal.

The mix of people on the beach was also very different. There was almost no one Darcy's age; most of the twenty- and thirty-somethings had been at work for hours. Darcy shared the sand with much older people. Retirees, she guessed. Many of them had dogs. They threw tennis balls and sticks and frisbees. They smiled at Darcy as she ran past, her unruly hair pulled tightly back, the sinews behind her knees elegantly taut. The older people seemed to take a quiet pleasure in her youth, and she in turn took comfort from their endurance and their calm.

There was something else about the older people on the beach at that in-between hour that Darcy had often noticed and often pondered: They were almost all women, and most of them walked alone.

Their aloneness intrigued Darcy and filled her with questions. Were these women divorced, widowed, gay and partnerless? Had they chosen their solitude or had it been imposed on them? Would they change their situation if they could? If they changed it, would they miss what they'd be giving up? Were they happy?

Running, keeping to that narrow ribbon where the sea foam dissolved and the sand was firm but not too wet, she let her thoughts meander. In recent days, of course, the more or less constant center of her reveries had been her father. But now she thought about her Mom.

Her mother, had she lived longer, might have been one of these handsome older ladies who walked the beach in solitude. Sheila Barnett had ended up alone, and that had been okay. Well, mostly okay. Eventually. But there had been a stretch when it was definitely not okay. Darcy wished she could forget that time, but of course she couldn't. Images from it dogged her even now as she ran along, surrounded by beauty, her body warm and buoyant with the simple joy of movement. Intruding on the bright morning were memories of her mother sitting in the dark alone; struggling to get out of bed and face the world again; seething with a hurt and disappointment that had nowhere to go but around and around inside of her.

Darcy ran harder, as if she could outpace the memories. She reached the pile of rock where she usually turned around, and she pressed on past it. Her pulse was racing now, her muscles screaming, her shoes biting deeper into the beach. She was both fleeing an emotion and chasing down a strand of logic, trying to pursue it to a resolution. What came to her at last, less a conscious thought than a feeling that had lodged in her sinews and her blood, was something like this: It was no catastrophe to be alone. It was only a disaster to be left alone. Which couldn't happen if one chose aloneness from the start.

Then again, was solitude really a cure for fear and troubling memories, or just a grudging stalemate with a set of riddles one had yet, on the cusp of thirty, to figure out? And besides, wouldn't it be nice to have someone running next to her on these gorgeous mornings, someone to leave his sandy sneakers beside hers on the mat?

This was a kind of thought she didn't very often allow herself, and it took her by surprise. She pivoted in the squeaking sand and headed home.

16.

Getting back to his feet on the giant lawn, Hugh Barnett had come to a decision. He tried to sound extremely steadfast and firm about it, but that simply wasn't who he was. The best he could manage was to say, "Okay, I'll try. Let's do it."

"Bravo," said his former wife. "Follow me."

She took off. She wasn't flying, exactly. It was more like she was floating, hanging suspended, while some vast and blurring backdrop was being furled behind her—furled so quickly and with such momentum that Barnett feared it would at some point snap and clatter like a sprung window shade. Yet, without apparent effort, he found himself traveling alongside her. He had no sense of motion except for a delicious fresh breeze in his face, like sailing upwind on a mild day.

At length the movement stopped. Barnett felt briefly wobbly, and when his equilibrium returned he had the sense that he was standing near a kind of seam. It was not exactly a horizon; it was not like the boundary between land and sea, or day and night, or any other margin he could think of. Still, it was a clear division.

Straddling the seam, spanning it and hanging over the far side, there was a diving board.

It was a quite ordinary-looking diving board, three meters high. Its stanchion was made of concrete, painted in a flaking, retro shade of aqua. The steps leading up to the board itself had metal treads. There were spindly handrails that did not inspire confidence.

Barnett said, "What the hell is that?"

His wife said, "It's your launch pad back to Santa Barbara."

"*That?* It looks like something from a third-rate swim club."

"You have complaints? You want a suggestion box?"

"It's just...Why is everything so low-tech around here?"

"Fewer moving parts. Less to go wrong." She gestured toward the board. "So are you going or are you wimping out?"

It was true that Barnett had been stalling. He'd always hated diving boards, ever since he was a little kid. He hated everything about them. The metal steps bit into his feet. The handrails were always cold and clammy, an echo of his fear as he climbed up. The rocking of the board had always made him sick to his stomach, made him feel that the solid world, as well as his own legs, had turned to gelatin. The worst, of course, was trying to look brave for the other kids.

Now he licked his dry lips, tried to swallow, and approached the board that spanned the nameless seam. He grabbed the handrails that were dry but chilly, and flashed a wan smile toward Sheila. She gave him back a neutral look that he chose to regard as encouragement. He started to climb, feeling the pattern of the metal step-treads in his feet. At the top of the stanchion he paused to look down. Only ten feet up, he felt as if he was clinging to the ledge of a tall building.

He said to his former wife, "I've got an idea. Why don't you come with me?"

She shook her head so that light spilled from it. "Can't."

"Can't?"

"Can't. Don't need to. Up here those two things are the same."

Happy to be chatting, happy to be stalling, Barnett said, "I don't think I understand."

"You've got things to settle. I don't. Not anymore. You can go because there's stuff you need to do."

"But wait—you said it's up to me if I go or not."

"It is. You don't want to go, come back down the ladder. But I'll tell you this. You're not going to feel terrific until you close out your account. And the longer you wait, it only gets harder."

Barnett pondered that, drumming fingers on the handrail. "You went back when you could?"

"This isn't the time to talk about it."

"But if you went, you could tell me what it's like. You could give me some advice."

Rather than answer, she made a little flicking motion with her hand, urging him onto the diving board. He shuffled along the plank and it trembled underneath him, whether in response to his weight or his shaking knees he could not tell. Halfway to the end, he felt an unexpected updraft; it was warm and fragrant, like a whiff of drying laundry, though in fact it exuded from a vent between worlds.

He pressed on along the yielding board, and just before the lip he hesitated one last time. Looking out, he saw nothing, not even darkness. Looking down, the same. No features, no contrast, no sense of good or bad or cold or hot or ending or beginning.

Even then he understood that he could turn around, backtrack down the metal steps, return to the uneventfulness and quiet of the boundless lawn. He didn't have to do this. Redemption, salvation—probably his wife was right to laugh at him for using those grand, pretentious words he didn't really understand. But at the very least, this was a choice.

He jumped.

Part II

Darcy and Paul and Sheila and Hugh

17.

In the loft apartment above his winery, Paul DeFiore was shaving.

He stood at a simple porcelain sink, above which a small frameless mirror was bracketed between two studs in a wall whose inside surface he had never quite got around to finishing.

Behind him, the main room of the loft, while tidy and efficient-looking, carried similar hints of incompletion and rough edges. The bed, though it had been neatly made, was nothing more than a mattress on a platform; the desk was a varnished wooden slab set on top of file cabinets. Around a switched-off computer were small stacks of order forms and invoices. Makeshift bookshelves held dozens of volumes of chemistry and viticulture, as well as assorted souvenirs—antique corkscrews, rusty shears, a threadbare Borsalino cap—of the harvests he'd worked during his interrupted apprenticeship in Italy and France. He wasn't big on daydreaming; didn't have the time for it; but now and then he found himself holding one of those mementos and thinking about the fresh, uncluttered life he'd had back then.

In distinction to the somewhat haphazard look of the living quarters, the winery below was immaculate. The walls were sheathed in redwood. Oak barrels were stacked in perfect pyramids. Brushed steel fermentation tanks softly gleamed, propped like rockets on their gantries. To anyone except Paul himself, the contrast between the downstairs and the upstairs would have been striking, its implications clear: Here was a young man who cared more for his work than his comfort. Or who, perhaps, still had much to learn about the value and nuances of comfort.

In any case, he stood there shaving, trying to psych himself up for the expedition ahead of him. He hated selling wine; he would have hated selling anything. How did you convince someone to like something? People liked it or they didn't. On top of that, Paul's wines were not what people usually expected out of California. They weren't soft and velvety fruit-bombs. They didn't gush with glycerin or seduce the palate with jammy sweetness. They were Old World style, restrained and lean. If people didn't care for them, fine; but Paul had sometimes wished they would at least consider that what they were rejecting wasn't just a beverage, but the entire purpose of what he was doing with his life.

Then again, wine was a business as well as a passion; and running a business called for thicker skin. Dragging the razor under his chin, he reminded himself to keep that firmly in mind. Making the list at a closely watched restaurant like Santa Bistro could only be a help.

Then again, selling wine was only part of the reason for this outing, and not the most important part; mostly just a ruse, in fact. He wanted to see Darcy again—though even now, as he was getting ready for the encounter, he wasn't quite sure why he was doing it. The ambiguity, in turn, was part of the appeal, part of the itch. He thought she was good-looking; of course he did. The firm shoulders, the graceful neck. He also liked her voice, which was soft and a bit wry, with a hint of questioning even when she wasn't asking a question. But everything he felt about her—whatever that was, exactly—was colored by the circumstance under which they'd met; a circumstance in which death was very close by. It was almost like the kind of whirlwind romance or near-romance that might happen in wartime—closeness accelerated by a crisis, then an abrupt and wrenching goodbye that left in its wake a dangling curiosity about what might have been. Curiosity—maybe that was it. Maybe as much as anything else, it was simple curiosity that made him want to see her again.

Not that seeing her again was necessarily a good idea. He had a vineyard that was just waking up from winter, and a mother who needed more help than she liked to admit, and a business that consisted, basically, of his energy and skill. Did he really have time for a romance? He'd tried in the past; the results had not been pretty. Then again, his life was busy but it was not complete; deep down, he knew this, though he generally tried to ignore or deny it. Something was missing; something was being stifled, albeit softly, like a face under a pillow.

He knew all this. But why should he think that any of it would change? Then again, if he didn't believe it could change, why would he be scheming to see Darcy again? Putting down his razor, rinsing away the last of the shaving cream, he couldn't think of one solid and persuasive reason--except that it seemed he simply could not do otherwise.

18.

Hugh Barnett had jumped feet first.

For a while, there'd been no sense of motion. There were no reference points to throttle past; no clouds slipping by or skyscraper windows streaking behind. But at some point, like an astronaut pressed back against his seat, he became keenly aware that he was accelerating. His lips stretched at the corners and his flesh strained outward from his cheekbones; he felt squeezed, foreshortened, shrunk down to the size and general contour of an egg.

Hurtling onward, helpless to slow himself or change direction, he sensed an imminent collision. The Membrane loomed before him, shimmery and opalescent, like the skin on boiled milk. At moments it appeared uniform and taut; then it seemed to flap and waver like a luffing sail. When he hit it, the sensation was less of an impact with something solid than a sudden and terrifying submersion in a sticky, viscous liquid. Although the Membrane was infinitely thin, Barnett felt that he was flailing through it like a panicked swimmer searching for the surface. The danger wasn't drowning; it was that he might dissolve—that his own containing edges might break down and the stuff he was made of simply ooze away, never again to be gathered into a self. But he held together and, at last, battered and exhausted, emerged on the Earth side of the Membrane, popping through like a bursting bubble in a pot of simmering soup.

Next thing he knew, he was at the end of Stearns Wharf in Santa Barbara.

The temperature was in the low seventies. There was a light westerly breeze, with just a hint of marine layer fog out toward the Channel Islands. In short, it was yet another replay of the same relentlessly pleasant day he'd reported on for decades. The only difference was that he wasn't there. Or not as a living person, at least. He was a disembodied visitor, a memory, a point of view. He could see but not be seen. He could hear but not join in the conversation. He could insinuate—at least his wife had told him that he could. But how?

He trusted that he'd figure it out, that the occasion would dictate the means.

In the meantime, he moved along the crowded pier. So much to look at! After the spare and monochrome ambience of the Other Side, the bustle and variety of Earth were breathtaking. People were fishing, gulls were squawking. Couples of every shape and size walked hand in hand. Tourists meandered in ridiculous hats, gazing at the boats, the pelicans, the little kids falling off of skim-boards. Boys with mullet haircuts and rivets through their noses strutted alongside girls with shredded jeans and studded eyebrows. In everyone he saw, Barnett sensed the capacity for joy, but also the undertone of struggle—the universal struggle to be oneself, to figure out a life, to decide where to place one's next footstep. It all seemed to matter so much, as if any tiny blunder—wearing the wrong shirt, uttering the wrong word—could poison a process that went on forever. People imagined that it *would* go on forever. This was the pressure of being alive. Barnett recognized it now with a compassion that had eluded him before.

He reached the foot of State Street. What a din! Compared to the quiet he'd already become accustomed to, even relatively placid Santa Barbara sounded like bedlam. Car doors slammed; motorcycles roared; somewhere a pneumatic drill was breaking up a sidewalk. Clashing music leaked from storefronts and blasted from passing convertibles; how did anyone think straight around here? Why did every person imagine that his own noise was necessary and meaningful, while the next guy's was mere annoying gibberish? Concentration, in the world of the living, was a triumph unto itself.

He wafted up toward the side street where Santa Bistro was. He was getting nervous; he couldn't deny it. He'd soon see his daughter. He didn't know how he'd feel. Earthly grief he understood; he'd felt it when his own parents had died, when Sheila was suddenly killed. But how would loss feel to a visitor from the other side? The dead, after all, had lost more than the living, and had lost it not one friend or loved one at a time but all at once. Now he'd be able to see Darcy but not to hug her, not to sit across a table from her and share some recollections and some laughs. He'd still be absent as well as present. And another thing: He had no idea how long he'd be allowed to visit or how many trips across the Membrane he'd be allowed to make. Sheila could no longer visit Earth; that meant that, for him as well, time at some point would run out once again, his business would be settled, and for him if not for his daughter there would be another excruciating parting.

Still, in the meantime he would see her, maybe even help her, maybe even make amends.

He drifted along the side street and over to the restaurant. Through its simple white curtains he could see that lunch was mostly finished. A few people were still sipping their espressos. A server was delivering a check; a busser was gathering up tablecloths.

Barnett screwed up his courage, passed through the plate glass window and floated through the dining room, then slipped beyond the swinging doors into the kitchen.

In Earth time, it had barely been a week since Barnett had seen his daughter, but his perspective was so radically different now that it seemed to him he must have somehow missed her growing up. His daughter! When had she become so adult, so capable—so much herself? He hovered near her as she worked; he longed to touch her shoulder, stroke her forehead, but touch was beyond what he could do. He lingered and studied her with awe. She was very finely dicing celery and carrots. Her fingers flew, her jaw was set in concentration. She was his daughter and she was also a separate human being. Why had this simple but overwhelming fact never struck him as quite this miraculous before?

The kitchen was buzzing. Steam was pulsing out of dishwashers, pans were being scrubbed in clattering sinks. While Barnett invisibly loitered, Nadine sidled over and stood next to Darcy. "Come on," she was saying, "join us. It'll be fun."

"I don't know. I don't really feel like it."

"Don't feel like tasting wine? Or don't feel like seeing the guy again?"

Darcy shrugged. She wasn't being coy. She truly didn't know. She said, "I think I'll just walk down to the beach."

"Fabulous idea," said her colleague. "Be alone with your dark and brooding thoughts when you could be here getting just very slightly buzzed with me. And break this poor guy's heart while you're at it."

"We've met exactly once. I don't think it'll break his heart."

Nadine lifted an eyebrow but otherwise let the comment slide. She moved on to a different tack. "Look, I could use your help, okay? I'm not familiar with these wines. I don't know how they'll work with the food. He uses grapes that hardly anybody uses. Italian stuff."

"I know. I've smelled it on his fingertips."

"You what?"

"Never mind."

Hugh Barnett, eavesdropping, had been floating underneath a rack of gleaming copper pans. Desperate to help, baffled as to how he could, he'd been waiting for an opening, a way into the discussion. Now he believed he had one. Italy. The opportunity was Italy. He did not *think* this, exactly; it would be more accurate to say that he became this thought. The thought ripened into a memory and rode a beam of emotion that swept through Darcy's mind.

Italy, Darcy. Remember? That trip we took when you were— what?—eight or nine? Mom had just gotten a promotion. We were celebrating. Stayed in nice hotels. Some mornings you got into bed with us and we all ate breakfast from a wooden tray. Everywhere we went, people made a big fuss over you, the way Italians do with kids. Remember how crowded the streets were? We held hands, the three of us, so no one would get lost. And it was the first place you ever tasted wine. Remember? You saw how the Italian families gave wine to their little kids—a few drops of wine mixed with lots of mineral water. Made a beautiful pink color. You wanted to try it, too. Your mother and I thought, sure, why not? You liked it from the start. Were very proud of yourself, clinking glasses and saying cin-cin, just like the grownups. The three of us, after that we always said cin-cin. Remember?

She remembered. She stared down at her cutting board, and when she lifted her face again, it featured a small, soft smile—a particular kind of smile that her friend Nadine had never seen before. "Okay," she said. "I'll stick around. Just for a little while."

19.

At four p.m. sharp, Paul DeFiore appeared in the empty dining room of Santa Bistro. He wore khaki pants and sneakers, a navy blue sweater over a pale blue shirt. He carried three bottles of red wine that had been uncorked, given an hour to breathe, then resealed with rubber stoppers. He shouted a hello toward the kitchen, and after a moment three people came through the swinging door—four, if you counted Hugh Barnett, who slipped through just before the rubber gasket collided with the opposite panel.

Leading the group was Scott Marsden, the owner of the restaurant. Fifty or so, trim, tan, and casually but expensively dressed, he'd made his money in other things, real estate and such; owning a restaurant was for him a bauble, a perk, a way to be visible as a local bigshot.

Behind him came Nadine. She'd put on street clothes and primped her spiky hair for the tasting.

Then came Darcy. She was still wearing her cooking clothes. This was not an accident. She'd been at pains to assure herself that this was not a date, but a business meeting at her workplace. So she would present herself as a cook, not a woman; in a role, not in the flesh. What she didn't realize or would not have admitted, however, was that she looked extremely fetching in her crisp tunic. Its simple line accented the well-toned breadth of her shoulders, the smooth arc of her collarbone. Like a perfectly neutral backdrop in a portrait, the white cloth lent a certain drama to her features, bringing out the green in her eyes and the flashes of rich red in her hair; her skin, glowing from her morning run and the heat and activity of the kitchen, seemed almost to pulse where it emerged from her loose collar or rolled-back sleeves.

Paul and Darcy's eyes had barely met, when Scott Marsden took charge of the proceedings, launching into hearty if not downright aggressive introductions. When her turn came, Darcy shook Paul's hand, trying not to think about his wine-stained fingertips, their lovely garnet color and their fragrance. "How's your Mom?" she asked.

"Doing well, thanks. Ahead of schedule on her rehab. Driving everybody crazy."

As if it was any of his business, Marsden said, "I didn't realize you two knew each other."

Darcy said, "We've met. Odd circumstance."

They moved toward a table that had been laid with a cheering array of wineglasses. Feeling suddenly bashful, afraid of getting cornered, Darcy maneuvered so she would not end up sitting next to Paul.

Hugh Barnett, meanwhile, hovered near the ceiling and tried to recoup his focus and his energy. He felt drained, sporadic, like a gizmo with low batteries. A demanding business, becoming a thought, transmitting a memory. At the same time, he was puffed up by his success. His daughter had somehow heard him. What else could he do?

Sitting, Marsden said to Paul, "DeFiore. Any relation to DeFiore's Foreign Car?"

"Yeah, that was my father's business. His *other* business, I should say. My Mom basically gave it to his chief mechanic when he died. Dad's dream, always, was to be a winemaker, but he had no capital to buy equipment. So the plan was to fix cars and sell grapes in the meantime, and save like crazy. But back in the sixties—"

"The sixties!" said Nadine. "No one was doing grapes here in the sixties."

"Exactly. My father was a pioneer." Paul heard himself saying this, and realized he was bragging about his father. This was not the first time it had happened. He vaguely wondered why he did it, why he felt the need. "That's why we got such a prime parcel," he went on. "Now we have Stolpman on one side of us, Jonata on the other. No way we could afford to buy there now."

"You could make a fortune selling," said Scott Marsden.

"I guess," said Paul. "But that's never going to happen."

Did Hugh Barnett imagine this, or was there something slightly wistful in the seemingly certain remark?

"Call me if you ever change your mind," Marsden said.

Paul let that pass. "Anyway," he went on, "back then land was cheap. Unfortunately, so were grapes. That's why my father started the car repair business. So he was a full-time mechanic and a full-time farmer. Do the math. Not quite enough hours in the day. Basically, he worked himself to death."

Scott Marsden said, "He should have planted Syrah."

Hugh Barnett, loitering above, thought *You asshole! This man is telling you his father's dreams, and you're telling him what kind of grapes he should have planted?*

Darcy, somehow sharing in the thought, just looked down at the table.

But Paul didn't bristle. "Syrah would've been an easier sell," he acknowledged. "Or Pinot Noir after the whole *Sideways* thing. Grapes go in and out of fashion, just like hemlines or hair-dos. But you plant, you wait, it's five years before you're making decent wine. What if you guess wrong about what's going to be in style five years later? Better just to follow your passion. That's what my old man thought, at least. Shall we taste some wine?"

He unstoppered one of his bottles and poured out four generous tastes.

"This first one," he said, "is a Dolcetto. Literal translation: *little sweetie.* The wine is dry, but what's sweet about the grape is that it ripens early and you can drink it young. In Piedmont, it's the common person's drink, while they sell the other stuff to foreigners. Relatively light, doesn't want a lot of oak."

Faces were turned down toward the handsome wineglasses. Everybody swirled and sniffed. The wine was tasted, rolled around over tongues and palates. For a few moments, no one spoke—the usual fear of saying something wrong.

Through the slightly uncomfortable silence, Darcy felt that Paul was looking at her over the rims of their respective glasses. Probably just waiting for her reaction to his wine. But she couldn't help feeling that the glance was something more than that, that he was sending her a particular greeting, reaching for a contact, an understanding, that would link the two of them and at least momentarily exclude the others in the room. The glance, she felt, was like a quiet invitation to step out onto a balcony for a breath of air and a few private words.

The attention was flattering. She tried not to notice that it was also exciting. It definitely made her nervous, and through the nervousness she heard herself blurt out, "Tastes like Italy."

A little snidely, though not without curiosity, Scott Marsden said, "And what's that supposed to mean?"

Surprised that she'd spoken, Darcy had no choice but to go on. "It makes me picture red soil and warm tile roofs."

"You taste roofs?" Marsden said.

"I didn't say I taste them. I said I picture them. But I can sort of taste the earth, the same clay the tiles are made of. It gives the wine a sense of place, a link to somewhere."

Hugh Barnett, swelling with paternal pride, thought, *You go, girl!*

Scott Marsden said, "I find it rather lean."

How poetic, Barnett thought.

"Well, that depends what you compare it to," said Paul. "It's not a typical hot-climate Syrah, that's for sure. I'm going for a bit less ripeness. Lower alcohol. Higher acid. Better with food, in my opinion."

"Be wonderful," said Nadine, "with charcuterie, sausage, anything informal and salty."

"How did Parker rate it?" Marsden asked.

Aha! thought Hugh Barnett. *The dreaded Robert Parker. World's most powerful wine critic. The final authority for those with no taste buds of their own.*

"He didn't."

"You don't even have a Parker score?"

"I've never invited him to taste it. Or any of our wines. My father..." Here he paused almost imperceptibly, dimly aware that he was about to praise his father, yet again, for a kind of stubbornness, a rigid certainty that had only made his own life harder. "My father," he went on, "had no use for critics. Don't let someone else's standards get in the way of your own. Don't pander and don't waffle. That's what he used to say."

"But without a Parker score—"

"I know, I know. It makes marketing more difficult. But—"

"Scores are stupid," Darcy said.

Even as she said it, she was a little shocked at her vehemence and her confidence, her sudden fierceness in taking Paul's side. Where were those things coming from?

"Customers like them," said her boss.

"Fair enough," she said. "But they just get in the way. They have nothing to do with what's special about the wine, with someone's experience in drinking it. How can you put a number on a wine? You might as well give a score to…to, I don't know…to making love."

Until the words were out, Darcy hadn't known she was about to say them. They silenced the room; they filled the silence. Darcy felt herself begin to blush. The blush was slow but epic, like the tide. It seemed to start from somewhere underneath her ribs, then surge along her neck, her chin, her cheeks, her scalp. Her skin prickled, her eyes itched. Her gaze turned shyly downward, but on the way it brushed against a look from Paul DeFiore. The fleeting glance made her feel as if he had touched her hair or grazed her face with his fingertips.

Scott Marsden cleared his throat and said, "Well, I didn't know you felt that strongly about it."

They tasted two more wines.

20.

While still lingering at Santa Bistro, enjoying the nearness of his daughter and the vicarious fellowship of wine, Barnett felt a sudden tug.

It wasn't like a familiar, earthly tug. It was not like a tug on the shirtsleeve, or even a tug on the heartstrings. He could not have said where the tug was coming from or what part of him was being pulled. In fact, it was his entire identity, his very existence, that was being yanked without warning away from the world. In a kind of instantaneous mini-death, he was being culled from the life around him, separated once again.

He could not have said if it was himself or Santa Barbara that was receding. He only knew that they were being pulled apart. For some instants, the distance between himself and life grew at a moderate, almost stately pace; he could keep the vanishing world in focus. But soon the rate of separation took an exponential leap; the world and everything in it fell away in crazy perspective, shrinking down to the size of a stadium dome, a basketball, a pea. When it had become the merest pinprick, faintly green, he saw the soft blue lights that signaled the Membrane.

Passing through it had not gotten any easier. Barnett hit it like a sparrow colliding with a car grille; the impact set off a flash of blinding white. After the crash, the Membrane seemed to turn into a sieve of infinite fineness; it filtered molecules, tested atoms, broke their bonds so that for a horrifying instant a person was like a disassembled watch, its lonesome springs and gears laid out on a workbench. The atoms—blindly groping, yearning—somehow found their partners, and a being, tuned up and disinfected, was recreated on the other side.

When Hugh regained awareness, he was standing on a featureless swath of the enormous lawn. His dead wife Sheila was next to him.

"So," she said, "it went pretty well down there."

Barnett couldn't answer right away. Everything seemed to be vibrating, thrumming. Like a person feeling seasick, he searched for a horizon to settle himself; but there was no horizon. After a moment, he said, "How'd I get back here? Did you yank me back?"

"Me? I don't have that kind of power. I do have friends in higher places, though. I can ask a favor now and then."

"But why so soon?" he grumbled.

"It always seems too soon. That's life. A hundred years would seem too soon."

He looked down at his reassembled feet, then at his former wife. He noticed, as he only half-consciously had before, that each succeeding time he saw her, her appearance seemed a bit more normal. She still had a pastel gleam around the edges; action lines still tracked her movements like phosphorescence in the sea. But her face had now become the face he'd known so long; her body had roundness and dimension. Studying her, he realized something else as well: There was a profound and almost shocking resemblance between Sheila and the daughter that she and Hugh Barnett had created.

It seemed crazy, but Barnett suddenly felt that he had never truly registered, certainly not acknowledged, the extent of this resemblance. Maybe, out of vanity, he'd been too intent on seeing himself reflected in his child. More likely, the resemblance had eluded him because, by the time Darcy had grown up into womanhood, he'd simply stopped looking at his wife. But now his view of her was fresh, renewed. He saw the thick, unruly hair that was so much like Darcy's hair. He saw the wide-set, alert eyes that turned down at the corners, the somewhat feisty chin, the expressive lips that, in life, had managed a hundred gradations between a smile and a frown.

He remembered after all this time that his wife was beautiful. The recollection baffled and embarrassed him. How the hell did a man forget something like that?

Trying to hide his discomfiture, he said, "I thought I was making some progress down there. I felt like I was helping."

"You made a good start. I admit it. The Italy thing—you nailed that one."

Barnett smiled, almost sighed. "It was a great trip, wasn't it?"

"Don't try nostalgia, Hugh. It worked with Darcy. It doesn't work for me."

"Okay, okay. But why couldn't I have stayed a while longer?"

"In Santa Barbara? To do what?"

"I don't know," he admitted. "But things were going well, they seemed to be hitting it off—"

"Which is exactly why it was time for you to leave. You can't force the tempo. Things move too fast, Darcy cuts and runs. You have to know when to back off. Besides, you only get a certain amount of time down there. I didn't want to see you wasting any of it."

"Wasting it?"

"Like, for example, by deciding to drop in on old girlfriends."

"Old girlfriends? I was visiting our daughter. Besides, I think you're overestimating me."

"No, it's been quite a while since I made that particular mistake. But come on, it was getting to be cocktail hour. Wasn't that the time you'd generally find some excuse to slip away? Share a bottle of chardonnay with some sweet young thing? Or maybe plant yourself at a bar and try to meet a new one?"

"For Christ's sake, Sheila, this again?"

"Why so touchy? It's in the past. It's from a different phase of existence."

"I just find the whole subject really unpleasant."

"That's a good one. A case could be made that *I'm* the one who should find it unpleasant, and it doesn't bother me at all. Why does it get you so worked up?"

He lightly slapped his hands against his thighs, kicked a toe against the featureless lawn. Finally, he said, "The truth?"

"No. Bullshit me, like before. Of course the truth. That's why we're here."

He hesitated, chewed his lip. "Okay. Here it is. I find the subject unpleasant because it makes me feel really lonely."

"Lonely? With all those adoring ladies doting on your suave manner and your television face?"

"Just for the record, there weren't quite as many adoring ladies as you probably imagine. But that's not the point. The point is that I ended up alone. That's what my suave manner did for me. I lived alone and I died alone."

"I hope you're not looking for sympathy."

"I'm not looking for anything. You asked me a question. I answered it."

Sheila's face changed. The change was subtle, barely noticeable, just the slightest shift in the angle of her lips, the depth of her eyes. Still, the change was striking because it was the first time there'd been any ripple at all in her serene expression. "I'll offer some sympathy anyway," she said softly. "Why not? Anyone who's ever been alive could use a little, right?"

Barnett couldn't meet her gaze just then.

"But I have another question," she went on. "Something I've never really understood. If you didn't want to be with me, why didn't you end up with someone else?"

For Barnett, the question didn't quite compute. "Who said I didn't want to be with you?"

Sheila, so much like her daughter now, gave her head a little shake and pushed back an errant wisp of hair. "Your illogic," she said, "is challenging my equanimity. Are you saying you *did* want to be with me?"

"You know, I've had a fair amount of time to think this over. And yeah, I really think I did."

"Then why—?"

"Why did I leave? Not because I wanted to. Not because I was running off with someone else. Because I was sick of the lying, sick of disappointing you, disappointing myself."

"There might have been another option," Sheila said. "Such as: stop doing what you were doing."

"Right. And give up smoking, too. Great ideas. I admit it. But what can I say? I couldn't do it at the time."

Sheila took that in. Her aura pulsed lightly, seemed almost to hum like neon.

"Look," her ex- went on, "I was just really bad at being married. I'm not proud of that, but there it is. And I think I finally figured out the reason. To be married—really married—you have to be able to say, Okay, this is my life. My only life. What's that line from the vows? *Forsaking all others.* That's not just about people to sleep with. It's about lives. Your own life. You're supposed to pick one, embrace it, be content with it. I couldn't do that."

"Our life was so bad?"

"Our life was terrific. A better life than I deserved. But that's not the point. The point is that I just couldn't accept the idea that it was the only life I would ever have. Maybe that's just another way of saying I couldn't accept that I would die someday. When I played around…You think it was about other skin, other bodies? No. I was kidding myself that I could have an extra life. That I could be someone besides who I was. Which is crazy. A farce, a total illusion. I see that now. But at the time…Does that make any sense to you?"

He looked up for her answer, but no answer was forthcoming. Sheila, long accustomed to taking care of herself, was discovering that her serenity was not quite as bulletproof as she'd imagined. Even for her, on certain archaic but tormenting subjects, the truth still hurt, and she decided just then that she needed to leave. She dimmed; she faded; she simply took herself away. The final words of Barnett's confession tailed off into empty space.

21.

"She said that?" asked Josh Traber, sitting at his usual place in the Café bar, sipping a glass of Viognier. It was dusk. The light outside the Café windows was lavender.

"Pretty much word for word," said Paul. "She said that giving a point score to a wine was like giving a score to making love."

"Well," his friend opined, "I'd say your tasting was a great success."

"And I'd say you're reading way too much into it. It was just a passing remark."

With enviable certainty, Josh said, "No it wasn't."

"Come on, you weren't even there."

"Right. But you were. Sitting just a couple of feet apart. She's sipping your wine, which you made with your own hands, into which you've put all your heart and soul. And right away she's comparing it to making love. Coincidence?"

Paul nipped at his wine. He was drinking a Grenache from the southern Rhone. It tasted of raspberry and pepper, and finished with a bracing hint of cedar. Rather stubbornly, he said, "It was just a figure of speech."

"Wrong. If that's all it was, there are plenty of other things she could have compared it to. Like giving a point score to a sunset. Like giving a point score to, I don't know, a puppy. But did she do that? No. She cut straight to sex."

Paul stared down at his glass. He both did and did not want to see it Josh's way. He could easily imagine himself as Darcy's lover—no problem there. He could imagine his hand twining through her thick hair, his lips against her forward-leaning neck…

Cutting through his friend's daydream, almost as an afterthought, Josh said, "And how did the wines go over?"

"Hm? Oh, pretty well, I think. The owner was a bit of a blowhard. Started in with the usual bullshit about Parker. The other chef, this woman Nadine, seemed to like them. Talked about food pairings right from the start."

"And your girlfriend? What'd she think?"

"She's not my girlfriend."

"Whatever. What'd she say about the wines, other than comparing them to fabulous sex?"

Paul paused to swirl and examine his glass before he answered. "Actually, the things she said about the wines, they were things you dream of hearing. No nonsense, no mumbo-jumbo. Just really from the gut. Like she was tasting not just with her palate but with her eyes and ears and memory. It was great."

Sounding almost envious, Josh said, "You really have to follow up on this."

"Easy for you to say."

"Yeah, it is."

The two friends sipped their wine. Behind them the Café was filling up. Dinner service was starting, plates were clattering onto tabletops. Behind the companionable curtain of sound, Paul said softly, "I did try to follow up."

"Excuse me?"

"When we finished tasting. It was sort of awkward. We all got up from the table. I wanted to talk to her alone. Just for a minute. Ask if I could call her, see her again. I couldn't get close to her. The owner had latched onto me, was telling some endless story. And Darcy—I really felt like she was trying to escape. Sort of hiding behind the other chef, slipping off to the kitchen. Barely said goodbye. It was a little strange."

Josh considered as he drained his Viognier. "No offense, but maybe she's just a cock tease."

"Possible. I don't think so."

"Scared herself, maybe?"

"Maybe."

"All that good stuff, then she barely says goodbye. That's tough to figure."

"Maybe too tough for me," said Paul.

In the kitchen at Santa Bistro, a somewhat similar conversation was taking place.

Doing dinner prep, finely mincing anchovies and salt-cured capers for a monkfish *provencale,* Darcy said, "I still can't believe I said that."

The comment was intended for Nadine, but Miguel, the pastry chef, who couldn't bear to be left out of kitchen gossip, intercepted it. "Said what?"

"Never mind," said Darcy.

Nadine was less quick to let it drop. "She said that rating a winemaker's wines was like rating how good he is in the sack."

"That isn't what I said."

"The guy I passed as I was coming in?" said Miguel. "That was the winemaker? Very cute."

Nadine said, "Forget it, Mikey. He's straight."

"All of a sudden you're the authority on heteros?"

She let that pass.

To Darcy, he said, "So what did you say?"

Looking down at her cutting board, she said, "Nothing. It was stupid. I don't even know where it came from. It just, like, flew into my head."

Nadine said, "Well, I thought it was great. Kept it real. Made Scott shut up about his precious ratings."

Waving a whisk, Miguel said, "Will someone just please tell me what she said?"

Darcy put her knife down. "All I said—and I meant it in a totally abstract way--was that giving an exact score to a wine was like giving a score to making love."

"That's abstract?" blurted the pastry chef. "Wine, sex, doing it—honey, that's about as concrete as it gets."

"The guy definitely appreciated it," said Nadine. To Darcy, she said, "Did you see the look on his face?"

Actually, Darcy hadn't. Not really. Recoiling from her spasm of boldness into a cramp of bashfulness, she'd looked straight down at the table. Her glance had slipped past Paul's like those of people riding opposing escalators, but there'd been no time to track the unfolding of his new expression.

Nadine said, "You could tell he was intrigued. Tickled. Curious. Like, what to make of it? It stayed on his mind. You could just tell. Like—what's that phrase?—subliminal seduction."

Miguel said, "Doesn't sound too damn subliminal to me. Sounds pretty much right out there."

"Can we please move on?" said Darcy.

Miguel wasn't quite ready to. "But this is so cool. So, what happens next?"

"Next?" said Darcy. This was one of her least favorite words, and it came out rather shrill and pinched. She picked up her knife and started furiously mincing. "Nothing happens next. There is no next."

As she was saying this, she truly believed it. There was no next because nothing had been started. And nothing had been started because, if there had been, she would already be prey to the worry and the sorrow of its ending. She'd spent a pleasant hour. That was that.

Her colleagues in the kitchen weren't buying it. They shared a certain look behind her back.

22.

Lolling around the infinite lawn, Hugh Barnett at some point realized he was hearing music. He could not have said how long he'd been hearing it, because the music seemed less an interruption than a crystallization of the perfect silence that had reigned before. The silence had been like a lake; somewhere it had flow and movement, but those things could not be seen or heard. The music turned the lake into a sea. Waves rose; currents merged and parted; the flow that had been there, hidden, all the while, now became a rhythm that was palpable. The silence had its pattern; the music had its pattern; each was as perfect as the other.

He could only guess the direction that the music was coming from. He turned his weightless strides that way. Even as he felt he was getting closer, he could not be sure if the music was coming from a single instrument, or several. At times the melody seemed simple, songlike, a tune meant for a single voice. But then it wound back on itself, shifted mood, seemed to reconsider. At moments the music was somber. But sometimes it seemed to be chasing itself like a dog in pursuit of its tail.

The music grew closer, the tone more incisive. Cresting a small rise on the rolling lawn, Barnett looked down toward a hollow and saw Manny Klein playing a violin.

The old man did not at first acknowledge his friend. He was rapt. His eyes were closed, his semblance of a body swayed and furled; he became a dancer led by the firm hand of the music. His fingers flew along the violin's neck; the bow blurred as it raked the strings. The music rose up one final time, paused as if to savor the view from a summit, and ended.

By that time Hugh Barnett was standing very close. "Bravo, Manny! That was beautiful."

Neither surprised nor unsurprised that Barnett was right there next to him, the old man said, "Bach. Greatest musical genius who ever lived. That, by the way, is not an opinion. It's fact. Fugue from the

First Sonata. How does anyone fit that much music into a piece for one lousy fiddle? Unbelievable."

"But the violin," said Barnett, pointing to the warmly gleaming instrument. "Where'd it come from?"

"I have no idea. I wished for it and it was there."

"Nice."

"Yeah. At some point I really had a yen to play again. I thought, Wouldn't it be nice to have a fiddle and some sheet music. The fiddle appeared, the music no. It was just like with the tea and the cookies. You get some of what you ask for, not everything."

"Better than nothing, right?"

"Funny thing, though. I found that here I didn't need the written music. If I could think something, I could play it. And without the sour notes. If I could've played that way when I was alive, I would have been Heifetz. Oh well. What have you been up to?"

Barnett hesitated, wondered where to start. Finally, he said, "I could tell you, but you'd probably think I was making it up."

"Try me. If I think you're a bullshit artist I'll say so."

So Barnett told Manny about his ability to travel back to Earth in the name of helping his daughter.

When he got to the part about his wife leading him to the diving board that spanned a seam in the cosmos, Manny said, "And you jumped? Without even seeing what you were jumping into? That took balls."

Pleased with himself, Barnett said, "I guess so."

"But it was worth it? You were able to help?"

"I made a start. I have a lot to make up for."

The two men fell silent for a while. Then Manny said, "But here's what I don't get. Who decides when you can visit? Who decides when you have to come back? Was it your wife?"

"I asked her that," Barnett said. "She can't do it on her own. She calls in favors. She has friends in higher places. That's all she'd say."

Manny scratched his neck, the side where the fiddle had been tucked. Softly, as if there might be eavesdroppers around, he said, "Are we talking God here?"

"I have no idea. God, a committee, I haven't got a clue."

The violinist pondered that, and after a moment Barnett went on.

"Look, here's as much as I understand. Sheila's at a different level than we are. I'd say a higher level, but higher, lower, who knows what any of that means? Anyway, she knows things I don't know, she can do things I can't do. Maybe it's because she was a better person. Maybe it's just to do with how long she's been dead. If I ever figure it out, I'll let you know."

Manny raised the violin as though he was about to play, then brought it to his side again. "How long's she been dead?"

"Nine years, give or take."

As if it were a mere coincidence, Manny said, "Same with Emma. Nine years, give or take."

The fiddle was still hanging at his side. With his left hand alone, he plucked at the strings. They made a plinkety-plink sound. Then he went on.

"I wonder if it's like high school."

"High school?"

"You know, you go in with a certain group of people, strangers at the start, no particular rhyme or reason, and that's your class. Some you like, some you don't. Some catch on to things, a few flunk out. Mostly, though, you're together straight through to graduation."

"Could be," said Barnett. "It's as good a guess as any."

"Then again," the fiddler mulled, "it could be based on merit. If you believe that people get what they deserve. But I don't know. You and me, we're here in the exact same place, even though it sounds like you were pretty much worse of a guy than I was."

"Thanks a lot."

"No offense. Besides, I think the high school thing makes more sense. Like, in the recovery room. You showed up, I showed up. There's only so many people they can process, right? Still, it's funny."

"What's funny?"

"That you and I end up in the same class, and your wife— what's her name again?"

"Sheila."

"That Sheila and Emma end up in the same class too."

Barnett shrugged. The happenstance did not impress him. In life there were many things that teased us with the promise of meaning, the goad of high purpose, but then turned out to be entirely random. Why should death be any different?

"You and your wife," said Manny casually. "You getting along these days?"

"Not really. Last time we talked, she walked out on me. I don't mean literally walked. She dimmed."

"Ah." The violinist tried to hide his disappointment, but he suddenly looked deflated, older. His white hair was very wispy and his posture had lost the improbable zip and elasticity it seemed to have when he was playing music.

"Why?" Barnett asked.

But Manny had turned shy. He waved the question off.

"Why do you ask?" Barnett pressed.

"I was just wondering...no, forget it, it's crazy. It's probably impossible. It's way too much to ask."

"Come on, Manny, spit it out."

"Okay. Okay. Do you think there's any chance at all that maybe your wife has run into Emma? That maybe she could help me find her?"

23.

By seven a.m. of the following day, Paul DeFiore was out working in his vineyard.

It was cold and humid at that hour; he could see his breath. When the sun finally climbed over the hills to the east, wisps of fog curled upward from the warming earth, slithering among the vines until they disappeared. The air smelled of dew and horses; a faint tang of iodine was carried by the day's first breeze off the ocean, some fifteen miles away.

It was early April, the time of bud break. Like everything else about a vineyard, bud break was miraculous. At that stage, the buds were nothing more than tiny, scaly bumps swelling along the shoots that had been pruned and trained onto their trellises in January; they were no bigger than a baby's fingernails. But from them—if the grower worked his tail off and Nature cooperated—would come the pendant cones of flowers that would then morph into tight, knobby clusters of hard and bitter grapes, which in turn would take on heft and sweetness and color in the sensual heat of July and August, and become new wine by autumn.

In the meantime, though, there was endless labor and worry and fretting to be done. Paul walked up and down the rows, examining each and every shoot on each and every vine. Here and there, a shoot had somehow shrugged its way off its cordon, and needed to be retied. Here and there a cane had twisted, hiding its buds from the sun. Squatting down, sometimes kneeling, ducking under strands of wire, he coaxed each vine into symmetry.

He was taking a break to stretch his back, when he happened to glance downslope and saw his mother working in her garden.

She wasn't supposed to be doing this. The tilt of the land and the hummocky soil threatened her balance; the step up to the raised vegetable beds was a taller step than the doctor wanted her to take. But at that stage of her rehab she had graduated from a walker to a cane. The cane left one hand free, and with that hand Rita was determined to work. She ripped the tatters of last year's tomato vines away from their supporting stakes, then tried to settle the stakes a bit more securely in the ground.

Paul jogged down from the vineyard. Rita gestured proudly toward the tiny section she'd cleared and broken up. "Nice, huh?"

"Yeah, Mom, beautiful. But come on. What if you hurt yourself? What if you fall?"

"If I fall I'll get up," she said, though she knew in her heart that this was mere bravado. This falling business—it was a nuisance, a humiliation. Since when was falling down a crisis? Since when was getting up again some great accomplishment? Toddlers fell down and got up fifty times a day. Boxers and football players got knocked down with great force; they got up almost every time. When did rising from the ground become such a big deal? Why did gravity have to pick on old people?

Changing the subject, she said, "Your tasting yesterday. How'd it go? Sell any wine?"

"They'll get back to me. The owner was a bit of a jerk. Gave me the usual line about critics' scores and using grapes most people haven't heard of."

Rita DeFiore shook her head and smiled. "Your father was a stubborn man."

"And he married a stubborn woman," said Paul.

He stepped up into the vegetable garden and started working next to his mother. This had always been her sole domain, but he didn't ask permission to enter it now. She understood his stratagem and appreciated it. If he had asked permission, she would have had to say yes or no, and the weight and fatigue in her limbs would have forced her to say yes. These concessions to age were galling enough without having to make each one a whole big discussion.

Besides, it was nice having her son so close to her. She cleared away the taller scraps and brittle stalks while he crouched low, pulling weeds. After a time, she said, "Your father's way of doing things, I sometimes wonder if he went out of his way to make life difficult."

"Why? Because he liked Italian grapes?"

"No, because he had a little bit of a chip on his shoulder. Let's face it. Maybe because, you know, he wasn't born here. He had to prove he could do things the hard way. Be as good as anybody else. Maybe a little bit better."

Paul kept his face turned downward and pulled more weeds.

"There were things he could have changed," his mother went on. "Where was the shame in watching what other people were doing, following what worked for them? Other people were selling lots of wine, getting write-ups—"

Paul interrupted. His own insistence took him by surprise. There it was again, the impulse to praise his old man--or to defend him, as the situation called for. He said, "Other people had their visions, Mom. Pop had his."

"And now you're stuck with it," Rita said. She said it lightly, wryly, but it struck Paul as a kind of accusation, not against his father but against himself.

Looking up, a clump of dandelions in his hand, he said, "Who said I'm stuck with it?"

"Not easy being the only child," Rita said. "A late-life baby, no less. I was forty when I had you. Very unusual for the time. We'd all but given up. We thought you were a miracle."

Paul kept weeding. He'd heard the story before, of course. It always made him uncomfortable. Who wanted to hear about his own parents trying to conceive?

Leaning on her cane, a stiff rake in her other hand, Rita scratched lightly at the ground. "A miracle," she repeated. "Your father would say *Miracle? That I don't know. But a son—a good son. That's enough of a blessing for me.*"

Paul said nothing.

His mother pulled at tatters of last season's plants. "And you *are* a good son," she said, as if someone had denied it. "But Paul, listen. I know how much you loved your father. But you don't need to keep doing things the way he did them. You really don't. He wouldn't ask that of you."

Paul was looking at the ground, shaking clumps of captured soil from the balled roots of a weed. He tossed away the stem and twisted his neck to look up steeply at his mother. "You really sure of that?" he said.

Darcy had woken up alone.

Neither part of this thrilled her—not the waking up part, not the alone part. The first few minutes of the morning were her least favorite time of day. Morning was a time of re-connection, of putting pieces back together, feeling welcomed back to life. But with no one at her side, who was there to do the welcoming? She threw back the covers, trudged to the bathroom, splashed cold water on her face, and got ready to go out for a run.

On the beach, now and then waving to one of the handsome, solitary, older ladies who were her morning allies, she soon felt better. Her body warmed, her mind cleared; she was reuniting with her own life. Her muscles stretched and pulsed as her feet plowed through the cakey sand; the endorphins kicked in, carrying with them a visceral optimism. Things were fine; she was fine. True, she rather suddenly found herself almost completely on her own. No family; not even a semi-estranged father. No lover; not even a casual romance. This was not the way she'd envisioned wrapping up her twenties. Well, there were things a person could control and there were things a person couldn't.

Lengthening her stride, tracing out the scallops of foam that spilled forth from every breaking wave, she reflected on her recent solitude. She'd been without a boyfriend for...what? Six or seven months now. It hadn't been the easiest time, but it was the right thing; she knew it was. It was a healthy pause, a cleansing. Not to mention a relief from the cavalcade of liars and knuckleheads who had gone before.

There'd been Dennis, a sandy-haired surfer boy who presented himself as mellow and spiritual, in respectful communion with the waves...until he'd had three or four beers, at which point he became bossy, argumentative, and crude.

There'd been Jean-Luc, a fellow cook—already a terrible idea— whose gaze was so riveting and who spoke so passionately about food and art and the graces of life, but turned out to be a total sleaze who was sleeping with a waitress on the side.

Most recently there'd been Charles, a somewhat older man, recently divorced. A successful attorney, so remarkably self-assured that he probably still didn't know why she'd finally broken up with him. Say this for Charles—he hadn't oversold what he was offering. He'd been married eighteen years; he wasn't ready to commit again. Fine, she hadn't asked him for a pledge of eternal loyalty. But how about just a little basic honesty and consideration? And why had it taken her nearly a year to understand that even that was too much to expect from Charles?

Those old boyfriends. They were all, at the end of the day, emotional lightweights, completely untrustworthy. Well, that was their problem. But Darcy had put up with them. That was hers.

The truth of this exasperated her; it was why she needed this time alone. She ran harder, as though she could outpace the troubling fact. Her boyfriends may have been guilty of this and that and the other, but that didn't mean she herself was blameless. Every bad relationship was a conspiracy. A liar needed someone to believe the lies, or at least to play along as if she did. Why had Darcy been so often willing to be that person?

She deserved better. She knew she did. But there was a world of difference between deserving something and actually knowing how to make it happen. Now there were this new fellow on the fringe of her world, this casual acquaintance, Paul. He seemed solid, kind, straightforward. But so had the others at the start. How could she trust herself to know if he was worth the bother or just another disappointment waiting to happen, another danger she should run away from?

Running away, she thought. It was actually sort of funny it should occur to her that way. Here she was, running in the sand, thinking about running from her past mistakes and even possible future ones; running away from bad choices she had made and the half-understood reasons she had made them. She was strong enough to run a good long way. But how long and how far did she really want to flee? Would there ever be an end to it?

Abruptly, she stopped. Hands on hips, breathing hard, she looked out at the green and empty ocean. No one swam this time of year, but in the next moment, without actually deciding, she knew that she was going in. She slipped out of her running shoes, pulled off her light vest; in her shorts and bra she stepped into the sea. The water was icy; it numbed her feet. But she pushed herself forward and when the surge was at her thighs she dove into a wave. The weight of it pulled back her hair; the salt put a light sting in her eyes and the suspended sand scratched at her skin. She swam a dozen firm strokes then rolled onto her back and blinked up at the sky. For a time she floated—not fleeing, not running, trusting the ocean to hold her safely up.

She jogged home barefoot, her body warming with each calm step.

24.

Emma Winthrop had summoned forth a cello.

In terms of simply making music, she didn't actually *need* a cello. Her neighborhood beyond the Second Membrane was a rather abstract and ethereal place, a precinct in which bodies were not necessarily required for the experience of pleasure and gear was optional for the exercise of skill. It could be pictured as a realm of shadow-boxers or silent, silhouetted dancers. Painters, if they chose, could conjure beautiful images without the need of paint or canvas; musicians could bring forth gorgeous sounds without the intermediaries of strings or valves or reeds.

Still, there were options available, choices to be made, and the cello Emma conjured was exactly like the ones she'd known in life. She'd conjured it because she wanted more than just the music. She wanted the friction of the strings against the pads of her fingers; she wouldn't even have minded a blister. She wanted the sometimes uncomfortable weight and knobbiness of the carved wooden scroll when she let the instrument rest against her shoulder. She wanted to remember what it was like to hit an off note now and then, to deal with the tiny emergency of adjusting pitch in the middle of a phrase.

She was feeling nostalgic for some of the richly textured imperfection of life, and she really couldn't say why. Something had been scratching at her mind, teasing her with memories of crossroads and decisions, flashing invisible postcards from a realm where mixed feelings were the norm.

So she swooped and leaned against the cello, pouring her subtle agitation into the music. Even as she played, she could not help wondering what her life would have been like—what her existence would be like even now—if she had done a few things differently.

Specifically, she thought about her marriage. It had by no means been a bad marriage; it was probably what would be called a solid marriage. It was based on sensible things like common interests, careers running more or less in tandem. It had lasted through the end of

Emma's life, and had never subjected her to the ugliness of violence or infidelity. The marriage had produced two healthy and accomplished children who had long before started families of their own. In all, it had been an appropriate and successful partnership.

Even so, Emma sometimes felt—and, mostly keeping it a secret from herself, had felt for many years—that something had been missing almost from the start.

Her husband, David—84 years old and still playing the occasional concert back on Earth--was a good man, probably better than most. He'd been considerate of her. He loved the kids. He was hard-working aside from being talented. Like everyone, he had his failings. He was very vain, especially in little things like hair and fingernails. He took himself a shade too seriously; maybe several shades. This, in turn, suggested the flaw—seemingly trivial in itself—that over time had sapped some of Emma's pleasure in life, that sometimes made her feel closed up and alone: David wasn't funny.

It wasn't so much that he lacked for wit, as that he saw laughter as a breach in the decorum he valued so highly. Life was serious; wisecracks were shallow. A man should be dignified; subversive comments weren't. Not given to laughter himself, David seemed—at least to Emma—to be critical of others' laughter. Not wanting to offend him, not wanting to seem childish or frivolous in his eyes, she'd censored her own humor and laughed less around him. Laughing less gradually became a habit; deprived of its necessary outlet, her more playful view of life began to be tinged with a solemnity that she knew, deep down, was not her own. It was an imposed solemnity, a hollow decorum. It came at the cost of denying a part of herself, and, inevitably, she grew to resent it.

Had she ever truly acknowledged this during her lifetime? Maybe not. It would have been awfully unsettling to do so. Besides, it was not as if David's relentless gravity was hostile or malicious; he was simply following the dictates of his temperament. Why hadn't she been equally insistent in following her own?

Leaning into the cello, rocking with the surge and backflow of the music, Emma allowed her thoughts to poke into holes and crannies that she'd regarded as forbidden for a very long time. She thought about her youth. She thought about dreams and doubts, about obligation and ambition and the confusing boundary between the two. She thought about decisions that had seemed to make themselves, crucial junctures where she'd veered this way or that. At the time, she must have been confident about the rightness of her choices, but now she couldn't quite remember why she'd made them. Or maybe it was that she no longer clearly recognized the young woman who had faced those decisions.

Although she didn't often allow herself this complicated luxury, she caught herself thinking about her first lover, Manny Klein. Manny...Manny was funny. With Manny she'd laughed at everything. If one of them missed an entrance in a string quartet, they laughed. Corny jokes on the radio, misprints in the newspaper, an absentminded professor with mismatched socks—they laughed. Why not? Where was the harm?

The laughing was the thing she most vividly remembered about her time with Manny, and she couldn't help wondering if this was strange. What about the lovemaking—her first experience, after all? She recalled that, too, with fondness, though in something of a haze of stubborn clasps and tangled underthings and worry about pregnancy and gossip. Could she truly remember Manny's body, back when he was twenty-two and lean and avid? Only in the most schematic sort of way. For that matter, could she recall or even re-imagine her own body in his arms—what she'd felt, how she'd answered his caresses? She supposed she could describe those things in words, but the sensations themselves seemed vague and far away.

Whereas the laughter seemed to be tickling her ears that very moment, winding through the music, punctuating the beats. It was what she remembered most intensely because it was what she missed the most. Wrapped around the cello, bending low for bold sweeps of the bow, she felt that she would gladly trade some measure of her not quite perfect serenity for one good, long, silly, unapologetic laugh.

25.

Paul DeFiore was working in his vineyard when Josh Traber came roaring over in his pick-up truck. He jumped down from the cab, shouted a hello, then reached into the back of the truck and came out with a wooden box. The box was painted white and had a screen on top. "Brought you some heavy-duty pesticide," he said to Paul.

Paul moved to lift a corner of the screen.

"Careful!" said his friend. "They look harmless but they're natural-born killers."

He put the box on the ground. It was full of ladybugs. Thousands of them, each one perfect with its humped, black-dotted body. Freed, they would spread out through the vineyard and gobble up the aphids before the aphids could gobble up the vine's emerging leaves.

Paul thanked Josh for the bugs and asked what he owed him.

"Forget it. Buy me a beer sometime."

"Fair enough."

Paul didn't exactly start to walk away, but he was already leaning back toward the row of vines he'd come from. He'd been banking small stones against the bases of the trunks; this was a trick he'd learned in Burgundy. The stones would hold the heat of the afternoon sun and make the onset of the evening chill more gradual, less jarring to the plants. It was tedious work but it had a rhythm to it, and Paul didn't like to stop in the middle of a row.

Still, Josh delayed him with a question. "So," he said, "have you called her yet?"

Distracted, his mind still on the stones and the vines, Paul said, "Who?"

"Who? Don't be a jerk. The chef who makes the sexy comments about your wine."

Paul produced a red bandanna from a back pocket of his jeans. Mopping his neck, he said, "No. I haven't."

"Why the hell not?"

"I don't know. Been too busy."

With his usual certainty, Josh said, "That's a load of crap."

"But it's spring."

"It's spring," Josh repeated. "Now there's a fabulous reason for not asking someone out."

"There's just so much to do up here."

"Right. Then it'll be summer, when there's even more to do. Then the September panic about rot. Then harvest, when you don't have time to scratch your ass. Maybe you'll have a two-week window to call her up next winter."

Paul looked at his vines. Giving up on the idea of getting back to work anytime soon, he sat down on the fender of Josh's truck. "Okay, here's the thing," he said. "This woman. Darcy. Say I call her. Something gets started. Then what happens?"

"How should I know?"

"Right. You can't know. And that would make me nervous."

"Nervous? How about intrigued? Excited? I mean, not knowing where it's going, that's part of the thrill."

Paul stared down at the dirt between his feet. "That's what I used to think. But other times…either the rug was yanked out from under me, or I just ended up disappointing someone."

"Ah," said Josh. "So you're just protecting the poor girl."

"I didn't say that."

"Like any woman you date is going to end up madly in love with you? Like she'll throw herself off a bridge if it doesn't work out? That, my friend, is total vanity and condescension."

"That's not what I—"

"Come on, give people some credit for knowing their own minds. Besides, all your noble bullshit, it's just a tarted up way of saying you're afraid of a commitment."

"Afraid of commitment? That's a good one." Paul gestured broadly across the vineyard and the winery and the house where he'd been raised. "You're looking at my commitment."

Josh weighed his words but didn't swallow them. "Due respect," he said, "what I'm looking at is real estate. It's a commitment, sure. But it's not a person. Whole different thing. How old are you now, thirty-three?"

"Thirty-four."

"Even worse. Come on, man, what are you waiting for?"

The question hung. The two friends looked at the ladybugs as they swarmed out of their wooden box. Some fluttered off to distant precincts of the vineyard. Some stayed close by and were already crawling up the rough trunks of the nearest vines, exploring every crease.

After a moment, Paul said, "You know, my parents were married for fifty years."

Josh just looked at him.

"Once or twice a year they had an argument. Screaming over something silly. You know, the typical Italian temper. Fifteen minutes later, they were back to holding hands. They were crazy about each other. Start to finish. How often does that happen?"

Josh said, "And this is why you won't call someone for a date?"

"I didn't say that."

"Because it might or might not lead to half a century of marriage?"

Paul kicked at the dirt.

"You know," Josh went on, "I've heard of people having trouble with relationships because their families were fucked up. I've never heard of someone being fucked up because his parents were too happy."

Paul took out the bandanna again, rubbed some dust from his neck. "I'm not fucked up, thank you very much. But what can I say— I'm just not good at doing things halfway."

"Halfway? You're worrying about halfway? You haven't gone *any* of the way yet. Will you please lighten up a little bit? Ask her for a walk on the beach. Lunch at the harbor. Something easy, something light. What's the huge big deal?"

26.

As Sheila Barnett saw it, it was in fact a big deal when Darcy and Paul finally arranged to see each other again.

She'd been monitoring developments. She was listening in when, a couple of days after his chat with Josh, Paul had finally beaten back his qualms and called Darcy. Still not knowing how else to reach her, he called her at the restaurant. He seemed to feel awkward about this and so did she. Their conversation was therefore terse and clipped. Not wanting to impose on her work time, his invitation to get together was blurted out without much grace. Protective of her privacy, not wanting to give her colleagues any more fodder for gossip or teasing, Darcy's acceptance had been bland and quiet, devoid of any obvious enthusiasm.

But Sheila had heard and felt far more than what was actually said in the thirty second conversation.

In Paul's reticence she heard the endearing, slightly tongue-tied struggle of a man who didn't ask women out that often and who didn't mess around. In Darcy's subdued response she sensed the off-note of a caution that did not come naturally, the residue of romances that had crashed and burned.

To Sheila it seemed clear that their mutual unease was a measure, a mirror image, of their mutual need. Both were powerful. Both were dangerous. If the fear prevailed, the love affair would be over before it started; there were always excuses to simply walk away. But what if the caution evaporated all at once and the yearning spun out of control? The result could be a passionate chaos, classic Darcy—a headlong leap leading to an inevitable thump, an audacious beginning that already held the seeds of an ending. Her mother felt the need for intervention.

In her neighborhood beyond the Second Membrane, there was very little difference between thought and action, and the recognition that her help was needed was enough to bring her to her former husband's side as he loitered rather aimlessly along the boundless lawn.

He looked up at her—at the by now familiar amalgam of light and flesh. He was neither surprised nor unsurprised to see her, but he was struck by a sweet though tardy thought: He remembered how much he enjoyed the mere fact of having her next to him. "Sheila!" he said. "It's good to see you. Last time we talked, the way you just disappeared—"

"There isn't time to go into that now."

Hugh went into it anyway. "You seemed upset."

"I *was* upset, okay? But that isn't what I came to talk about."

"I'm sorry I upset you. But...wasn't it sort of nice?"

"Nice?"

"That we could talk like that. That we still care about each other."

"Who said that?"

"Come on. Why else would you walk out?"

"Don't flatter yourself, Hugh. I walked out because...because, listen. One of the advantages of being dead is that you have the luxury of believing you finally understand things. It's like the movie has stopped. You can go back and look at it frame by frame. I thought I understood why our marriage ended. Then you hit me with this whole different spin on it. It was unsettling, that's all."

Barnett said, "I didn't think you could be unsettled."

Sheila said nothing. He tried to look into her eyes but she had turned them down and away from him.

"You once told me," he went on, "that, around here, you can get to a place where everybody tells the truth because the truth no longer hurts."

"Right. But I never claimed I was there yet. And I didn't promise that you would ever get there, either. Look, we're deceased human beings. We're defunct. We're out of business. But we're still human. Sort of. That's the tricky part. But enough about us."

"Us? You called us *us!*"

"Forget it, Hugh. I didn't mean it that way. I'm here for Darcy. She's about to go out on a date. They're not calling it a date. But it's a date."

"The winemaker?"

Sheila nodded.

"Oh shit."

"Oh shit, what? I thought you liked him."

"I do. He's fine. It isn't that." Barnett hesitated, looked down at his feet. "I have to go?"

His former wife seemed a bit confused. "You don't have to do anything. But what's the problem? Last time you went, you said you felt good about it."

"Yeah. I did. But that doesn't mean I want to go again."

"But if—"

"I guess it's like you said. We're still human, sort of. I see Darcy, it hurts. Then I have to leave, and it hurts again. The leaving—it wears you down."

Sheila said nothing. She had an impulse to touch him on the shoulder but she was afraid he would make too much of it and so she didn't.

After a moment, Barnett said, "But, okay, here we go. Bring me to the diving board."

With a resolve flawed only by a few brief moments of stalling, he climbed the metal-treaded steps and gingerly walked the length of the board. He crossed over the vent in the universe, felt the warm and humid updraft; the board rocked just slightly, like a gently rolling boat, beneath his negligible weight.

He paused. Knowing what the journey back to Earth was like did not make the leap any easier. He dreaded the sickening acceleration in the instant before he hit the Membrane. He quailed at the memory of the impact, the terrifying sense of drowning in taffy. Most of all, he shuddered at the prospect of being dissolved and reassembled, of his identity being shredded as though it were a guilty document.

He stepped off the board and let himself go.

The passage was grueling. But…did he only imagine this, or was it somewhat less so this time? Was it conceivable that the journey had gotten at least a little easier because there were fewer lies to scour away, fewer illusions to be blasted, a slightly less dirty conscience to be scrubbed? Was it possible that Hugh Barnett was actually making progress? Then again, how many sieves and strainers would it take to filter every last bit of regret and ambivalence from a human life? Probably more than could be counted.

27.

For quite a few years now, Paul DeFiore had ironed his own shirts. He took pride in this even though he wasn't especially good at it. When Paul ironed a shirt, it generally ended up with a pucker in the collar or an unintended crease down the back. On the shirt he wore today—a pale blue and green tattersall plaid—there were little crinkles in the placket. He hadn't really noticed them and he wouldn't have known how to fix them if he had.

He was sitting on a bench next to the bike path that wound along the splendid beach that stretched from downtown Santa Barbara all the way to Montecito. He seemed a little nervous; he crossed one leg, then the other, each time grabbing an ankle and fussing with his socks. From where he sat, there was much to look at—joggers, skaters, tourists pedaling by in clattering surreys with yellow canvas tops—but after each brief distraction, his gaze turned again, expectantly, to State Street.

At some point, Hugh Barnett was hovering next to him.

The former weatherman had landed just at the edge of the water. Somewhat like a wet dog, he'd given himself a shake to refresh his dignity and get his bearings, then, by reflex, he'd made a note of atmospheric conditions—temperature in the seventies, marine layer out toward the islands. What else was new? He'd drifted over toward the young man who was waiting for his rendezvous with Darcy.

As Paul waited, Barnett remembered, from his own life, the sweet suspense of waiting for a desired woman to appear. Given his history of philandering, he had many such trysts to reflect upon; somewhat to his own surprise, however, he found himself thinking only of the times he'd waited for Sheila, back when they were courting. Often, she was ten or fifteen minutes late. A conscientious assistant way back then, she was always putting out other people's fires or rewriting some messy copy before she left the studio. Barnett didn't mind her tardiness. It was a pleasant tease, a species of foreplay. It gave him time to wonder what she would be wearing; to try to recall exactly the mix of colors in her eyes. It allowed him to place himself strategically so he could savor the sexy privilege of watching her for a moment before she knew that she was being watched.

The dead man, then, understood why the living one kept shifting on his bench, kept plucking at his socks. This was how it was with new, uncertain lovers. It hadn't changed. It never would.

After a time Darcy appeared.

She was on the far side of the road that paralleled the beach, waiting for the light to turn green. She wore khaki pants and a marine blue sweater with a boatneck collar. The garment's color contrasted smartly with the red glints in her hair; the neckline traced out the graceful arc of her collarbones and the feisty tilt of her shoulders.

Paul rose as she approached. Her father wondered if they would hug, kiss on the cheek. They shook hands. *So careful!*

"Thanks for meeting me," Paul said.

"I was glad you called. Probably didn't sound that glad. Sorry. You know, work and all."

He nodded. "Shall we walk?"

They set off down the bike path. They didn't hold hands, didn't put their arms around each other. But now and then, when a cyclist or a jogger was passing them by, they squeezed together so that their sides were touching. Sometimes Darcy took Paul's arm to coax him out of a skater's path; sometimes Paul put a hand on Darcy's back, guiding her around a knot of tourists.

Scudding on the ocean breeze, Hugh observed and tried to remember—*really* remember—the sensation of touch. What a privilege and what a mystery it was that two people, strangers, could craft a bond, could discover affection, from the fleeting contact of fingers and palms, from a considerate press between the shoulder blades or a helpful tug on an elbow. These small exchanges of touch were a conversation of the skin, every bit as telling as a conversation made of words. Like every other sort of interchange, the conversation of touch flowed or it did not, felt genuine or forced.

After a while, Darcy said, "How's your Mom? What's the latest?"

"The big news? Her tomatoes are in. Other than that, she thinks she's hiding it that she still has pain. I act like I don't notice. But all in all, she's great."

They walked. Little by little they relaxed. Waves hissed softly as they broke and turned to foam.

Paul said, "And your father. What happened. We never really got to talk about it. Do you want to?"

Darcy looked off toward the seam of beach and water. "I guess that would be good. I haven't talked about it much. Not out loud, at least. It's amazing to me that it's almost a month already."

Hugh Barnett stopped short in his scudding. *A month! I've been dead a month? It feels like about two hours. Wow. I guess that's why they call it eternity.*

"The way it happened," Darcy went on. "The suddenness. It just threw me for a loop. I wasn't ready for him to be gone. I mean, it was a pretty routine surgery."

"I wonder if anyone's ever ready."

"Probably not. But you know, there was just so much we didn't get around to saying, working out. I'd been angry with my father for a really long time."

"Because he left?"

"I told you that?"

"About twenty seconds after we met."

"Nice that you remember. But no, that wasn't it. Not really. People have a right to make themselves happy. If he wasn't happy, he was right to go. What bothers me is the stuff that went before. The lying. The sneaking around. Did he think I didn't notice? Come on, kids figure out what's what."

(Drifting through the salt air, Barnett cringed. Had he really been so obvious? How long had his little girl seen him as a cheat? When was it that he first let her down?)

"But the thing is," Darcy went on, "even when I was the most pissed off at him, I always sort of thought it wouldn't be forever. Somehow we'd get past it, the grudge would go away like...like, I don't know, like baby teeth falling out or a cast coming off a broken arm. Something you get over, and it's done. Does that make sense to you?"

Paul gave half a nod and half a shrug. "I guess, but—"

Relieved to be talking, Darcy soldiered on. "My feelings for him were always so extreme. I was so proud of him when I was little. He was handsome. He was charming. He was on television every day. To me he was like a movie star."

"Nice to have those memories," said Paul.

"It is," said Darcy. "It is. Except…"

She suddenly stopped walking. She just seemed to need a moment to stand still and neither speak nor hear a word, to drop her eyes and look at nothing and let her hands hang at her sides.

"Except," she went on, "now that he's gone, what do I make of this man I adored, who turned out to be a liar and a cheater and who spoiled everything?"

She looked up at Paul. She tried to smile but her brow was taut and her eyes gleamed at the corners. Gulls screeched. Waves sizzled over stones. Paul reached out very slowly, as if trying not to startle a bird, and put his arms around her. She let her cheek rest against his shoulder, then brought her hands up to his back. The hug did not last long—two or three breaths in which their bodies filled and emptied in rhythm, in which they felt the tickle of each other's hair. The embrace ended in shy smiles, not a kiss.

Darcy's father hovered above them, rattled and ashamed. He deserved to hear the things his daughter had said; he accepted that. Still, what was the purpose of the chastening? Was he there to help, or only to suffer?

28.

When they started walking again, everything was different.

To Darcy, the difference at first felt like a comfort. A barrier had been broken down, an obstacle surmounted. Paul had heard her out with close attention and answered with kindness; she'd felt snug and safe in his arms.

But that, of course, was the problem. The hug had felt too good, too right, and within moments Darcy had started to mistrust it. Who was this person? Why should she imagine that his tenderness would last? The feel of that hug—it was something she could easily get used to, even come to need. What if it was then taken away? Fear of betrayal put a milky feeling in the pit of her stomach and climbed up beneath her ribs, unstoppable as nausea. She felt loss in advance; she felt the secret fury that goes with loss. Absurdly, she was ready to be angry with Paul, as though he'd already transgressed somehow, already let her down.

She felt like she needed to flee. Her mind racing, she searched for some excuse, any excuse, to bolt. Or maybe she'd just walk away without a word, vanish before there was yet more emotion and more hope for her to leave behind.

Her father sensed her rising panic and understood that he himself was the cause of it. Grappling against his own hurt feelings and his shame, he tried desperately to figure out a way to help. It had to happen quickly. Time moved so fast here on Earth. Moments flickered by as if shot from a strobe; chances for happiness flashed and disappeared like meteors. Hugh Barnett focused with all his might and sent his daughter a memory—a memory from the time before he had begun to disappoint her.

It was a memory of clouds.

Darcy, maybe looking at the clouds will calm you down. I used to bring you to this beach, remember? We'd sit on a bench or sometimes on a blanket. We'd look at the sky, and I taught you the names of the clouds. Cumulus—those fluffy white ones that sometimes took the shape of animals or states. Altostratus—slow flat clouds that spread across the sky like syrup.

There was a trick I used to play on you. I'd point to a wispy cloud and tell you I could make it disappear. Then I'd put my hands over your eyes, and when I took them away again, the cloud would be gone. I think you knew I didn't really make it disappear. It melted in the sun. But you liked having my hands on your forehead, covering your eyes. What trust!—to let someone cover up your eyes. Nothing bad happened. Remember?

Pushing back against her fear, working hard to control her stride and to make her voice sound normal, Darcy said, "Mind if we sit a minute?"

They'd walked, by then, as far as the old bathhouse. They sat on a low wall that was warm against their legs. Darcy looked off toward the south and pointed to the sky.

"Those feathery little clouds?" she said. "Those are cirrus. My father taught me that. Other places, he used to say, cirrus clouds mean a change in the weather. Here they don't seem to mean anything. But they make for beautiful sunsets. They're made of ice crystals. They get green then yellow when the sun goes down."

Paul stretched his legs and let his heels fall softly back against the wall. "Your father teach you a lot about the weather?"

"Just basic stuff. Cold fronts, warm fronts, how the jet stream dips down like a giant spoon in winter. A lot of it I don't remember. Can I ask you a favor?"

"Sure."

"You won't think I'm crazy?"

"Depends what the favor is."

She reached down and took his hand. The palm was very soft, though the fingertips were scratched and thickened from the constant work in the vineyard; the cuticles were still tinted garnet from the strong pigments of wine. She said, "I'd really like it if you'd put your hand across my eyes. Just for a few seconds. Just for a few deep breaths."

Paul hesitated.

"Like this." She lifted his hand, splayed out his thumb and forefinger just above the sweep of her brow. Gently, she coaxed his hand down like a shutter on a window. At first she didn't dare to close her eyes; she squinted at the pink slices of light that slipped between his fingers. But then she let her eyelids fall. She entrusted herself to the darkness and the warmth of Paul's hand on her forehead.

She opened her eyes. He slowly pulled his hand away. They smiled at each other, and she knew that it was time to go. But now she wasn't fleeing; rather, she was trying to preserve a feeling, capture that moment and lock it safely away.

Without a word, she stood. Turning to Paul, she gave him the quickest and most ambiguous of kisses. It was more than a peck on the cheek. It was less than a kiss on the lips. It landed just at the corner of his mouth, so light and fleeting that he needed to remind himself that it had actually happened.

She turned away from the beach and headed toward the street.

Part III

The Angels' Share

29.

Before Darcy reached the crosswalk, her father had once again been yanked from life, shredded by the Membrane, and reassembled on the other side.

Sheila was there to meet him when he arrived, frazzled and jittery, back on the boundless lawn. "So how'd it go?" she asked.

"I felt terrible," he said.

"I didn't ask how you felt. I asked how it went."

Barnett ignored the distinction. "I felt about this big. Darcy knew about my cheating all along. From, I don't know, from when she was a little kid."

"You're surprised? You think your daughter's stupid?"

"Of course not. But I thought…I thought I was being so clever, so smooth."

"Apparently not."

"She saw right through me. She figured out so much. A whole lot more than you did."

"Embarrassing but true," Sheila admitted. "Willful blindness. That was me. But then, you didn't work as hard at hiding things from Darcy. But enough about you. Tell me about the date."

"You didn't see it for yourself?"

"Of course I saw it. I see everything Darcy does. But I'm asking your impression."

"I thought it went pretty well."

"Such insight!" said his wife. "Such mastery of the telling detail."

Barnett toed the lawn and considered. "Okay, okay. You want insight. Here's my insight. I think Paul's a really nice guy, and I can't help being concerned that maybe Darcy's a little too wiggy for him."

"Darcy's not wiggy."

"Come on, I thought we're telling the truth here. I say this with love. I say it with guilt. Our daughter's a little wiggy."

"And you don't think he's intrigued by that?"

"I *do* think he's intrigued. Definitely. But it's a fine line between being intrigued and being driven crazy. And I don't think he's a guy who'll let himself be driven crazy."

By reflex, Sheila became protective of her daughter and instantly dismissive of anyone who might let her down. "Well, if he's ready to give up so easily, then the hell with him."

"Wait a second. Who said he's ready to give up? I never said that. And why are we arguing about this? I think we're on the same side here."

Sheila paused. Her glow pulsed and dimmed in an abstract version of a shoulder shrug. "Okay. You're right. I don't know why this is, but the last couple of times we've talked, I've gotten all worked up."

Barnett put on what he believed to be his very most charming smile. "Because you still care," he said.

"Lose that idea, Hugh. This is totally about Darcy. You know what it is? It's that I can't help as much as I want to help. I see everything and can change nothing. It's very frustrating."

"Kind of like being a living parent," said her former husband.

"A lot like that, I'm sorry to say."

For some moments they just stood there on the lawn. They could as easily have been a divorced Mom and Dad summoned to a conference with their seventh grader's principal, struggling in the face of grudges and resentments to be allies for the sake of their child.

Finally, Barnett said, "And listen, while we're here, there's someone else I'm hoping we can help."

Relieved at the change of subject, Sheila said, "You're quite the do-gooder all of a sudden."

He let that pass. "It's for a friend."

"You have a friend? Around here? What's her name?"

"Come on, it's a guy. We met in the recovery room. Next bed over. Probably just coincidence."

"Probably not. But go ahead."

So he told her about Manny Klein, and his youthful love affair with Emma Winthrop; and their parting in the name of what they thought was responsible adulthood; and of him pining for her for more than half a century.

"He never got to see her before she died. Which was right around the same time you did. Maybe that's not a coincidence either."

"Probably isn't," she conceded.

"So maybe you could find her. Any chance? It would mean an awful lot to Manny."

"Hugh, do you have any idea how many beings are fluttering around up there?"

"I'm sure there's lots. But how many of them are lady cellists?"

"Okay, okay. I'll see what I can do."

In the kitchen at Santa Bistro, Darcy had an inspired but erratic evening. Her knife work was a blur of speed and precision; her plate arrangements were painterly; with no visible effort, she whipped up a béarnaise that had the mystic shimmer of medieval glass. Amid those triumphs, she also managed to burn a rib-eye steak and to botch a simple swordfish with aioli. Now and then she found herself humming.

At the end of dinner service, Nadine said to her, "What is what, girl? You cooked tonight like you're in love."

"Let's not even go there," Darcy said.

"Oh, so I'm not far off."

Darcy said nothing.

"That winemaker," Miguel put in, as he dried his whisks and hung them carefully on pegs. "I'll bet you it's that winemaker. How tight were his jeans?"

Darcy once again said nothing.

Nadine said to Miguel, "Why is it always the jeans with you?"

"With me?" he said. "With everyone. I at least admit it."

Darcy let them banter and quietly went about her work. She was trying to hold on to certain moments, certain feelings; she didn't want them to evaporate into mere words, didn't want them to drift away on the breath of casual chit-chat.

But on the drive home to Carpinteria, her demons started grumbling and her thoughts became a muddle.

She tried to remember the feeling of Paul's arms around her, the look in his eyes when she'd told him things that were difficult to talk about. She tried to recall the exact sensation of their quick kiss and to recapture her own boldness in starting it. But along with the pleasure of revisiting those things, came an upwelling of worry, of the perverse but familiar dread that she couldn't seem to shake. What had she started? What if Paul was not as solid as he seemed? What if they became lovers and it was truly wonderful? What if it wasn't? What if he cheated? What if he left?

She tried to stop the thoughts, but they barreled along like the traffic on the freeway, now racing, now clotting in slow and maddening clusters. Things had a way of ending badly; pain was proportional to caring. She felt the old impulse to bail, to cash out before she'd risked too much. She remembered Paul's hug and wished she could let herself melt into it forever. She also wished the hug had never happened.

At home in her apartment, she poured herself a glass of chardonnay and eased into the gradual process of winding down toward sleep. At some point she noticed that her answering machine was flashing.

She pushed the button and from the first syllable she knew the message was trouble. She might have stopped the playback, but she didn't; she listened to the end.

The message was from Charles, the co-conspirator in her most recent bad relationship. He said he'd seen her on the beach that afternoon. He'd jogged past while she was deep in conversation and she hadn't even noticed him. But seeing her again made him realize how much he'd missed her. Could they get together? Could they have dinner sometime soon, try again to make it work?

The long and purring message ended with a beep. The indicator light still winked at Darcy, suggestively, subversively. She told herself to erase the message and forget about it. She was done with Charles. She hadn't wanted to hear from him. The timing of his call was horrible. Or perfect. Paul scared her. More to the point, in Paul's company she scared herself. Charles, a charming lightweight, didn't scare her in the least. He'd never offered very much, but they'd had some good times together; besides, now, belatedly, he *was* offering something that tempted her--an easy out from her anxiety, a relatively painless, backsliding exit. She'd be disappointed in herself if she took it; she was totally aware of that. But maybe she'd rather be disappointed in herself than risk being let down by Paul.

Then again, her ferocious morning runs; her freezing, scouring swims; her months of self-imposed loneliness—what were they for, if not to help her move beyond her fears, bust out of old mistrustful habits, get ready for something fresh and wonderful?

That was it--she would erase the message. She reached out a finger; it stalled on the way to the button. She couldn't quite do it. She wasn't quite ready. She'd sleep on it, decide tomorrow. The message stayed in the machine, invisible but lurking, like a spider in a box.

30.

The next morning, Paul DeFiore was out in his vineyard, working and worrying.

Frail new leaves had begun appearing on the green shoots. When they first emerged from the scaly buds, they were all curled up like newborn kittens, and they were vulnerable to everything. A late freeze could burst their veins and turn their substance to mush. A passing horde of insects could gnaw them to the quick. A freak hailstorm could leave the whole vineyard shredded in two minutes.

At this time of year—even more so than at all the other seasons--Paul felt a compulsion to be with his vines at every possible moment. Could he have stopped the frost if it came rolling down the hillside? Absolutely not. No more than he could have singlehandedly chased away a plague of grasshoppers or fended off a flood. Still, this vigilance, this watching over, seemed absolutely necessary to him. He'd seen his father do it every spring. The vigilance was as much a ritual as a chore, as much a humble acknowledgment of helplessness as an active part of farming. Frank DeFiore had seemed to believe that his unwavering attention had a power that could not be reasonably explained in words. The power was almost like that of prayer, of exhortation, and Paul, secular and skeptical though he was, had nearly come to believe in it himself. Somehow it added something to the finished wine.

Squatting down between two rows, gently wrapping an errant shoot around its cordon, Paul did not immediately see his mother walking toward him. She'd grown somewhat less reliant on the cane, though she still leaned on it as she picked her way along the yielding and uneven ground. When she was just a few yards from her son, she ran her fingertips along a trellised shoot. "The buds look great this year," she said. "It's going to be a terrific vintage."

"You can tell so early?" Paul asked. They both knew perfectly well that no one in the world could tell so early.

"I can tell," said Rita. "Or I can hope at least. How's that?"

She smiled at her son. Her eyes crinkled up at the corners and Paul could see that they were slightly red and swollen. "You okay, Mom?"

She tried to hold the smile, but it got away. She said, "I'm a little blue, is all. Happens around this time of year. Around the anniversary of your father's death."

Abashed, Paul said, "Seven years, right?" This was not really a question. He knew for certain it was seven years. "I really should remember the day."

Rita shrugged. "Your father wouldn't want you to waste your time remembering. He'd want you to be doing exactly what you're doing."

Paul was still squatting down, fussing with the vines. He turned his chin up toward his mother. "You say that like you're pretty sure."

"I am."

"How do you know?"

"I just do."

"But how?"

Rita said nothing.

"You talk to him? He tells you things?"

She lifted up her cane and pointed its rubber tip at her son. "Okay, make fun of an old lady. That's fine. As a matter of fact, I do talk to him. Every day. So what are you going to do, commit me? I happen to believe he's still in touch."

"Okay, Mom, whatever gets you through." He continued with his work, but after a few moments he realized he had gotten curious. "So, like, what do you two talk about? What does he tell you?"

To her son's surprise, Rita suddenly seemed shy. "Just this and that. Everyday things. The weather. What's for dinner. How I'm doing. How he's doing."

"Really? And how is he doing?"

Paul's tone was playful, gently teasing. But his mother did not answer in kind. Her eyes turned away and she seemed a little sorry to have raised the subject. "It's not for me to say. Sometimes it's troubling. He has his problems, too, you know."

Caught now between banter and a growing concern about his mother's state of mind, Paul said, "No. I didn't know."

"He doesn't talk to you?" asked Rita.

"Mom, you're weirding me out a little bit. Do you mean literally talking? Or just remembering? Do I picture Dad sometimes? Sure. Can I hear his voice? Of course. But that's just memory. I mean, it's not like he's talking to me now."

Rita scratched at the ground with the tip of her cane. "Okay. I'm sure you're right. It's just memory. Imagining. But what's the harm?"

"No harm, Mom. Sorry if I made it sound that way."

"It's just that sometimes," Rita said, "it really seems so real."

31.

Sheila Barnett, her gleam somehow disheveled, flashing here, glaring there, suddenly appeared again on the rolling lawn. Before her former husband could even say hello, she said, "Hugh, we have to talk."

"You found the lady cellist?"

"I'm working on it. But that isn't why I'm here. We have a crisis.

That shithead Charles? Darcy's last crummy boyfriend? He's gotten back in touch with her."

"That lawyer? The older guy? He's a total liar and a snake."

"Wonder who he reminds her of."

Barnett grit his teeth but let it pass. "I thought she dumped him months ago."

"She did. Apparently he won't stay dumped. He saw her on the beach the other day and called her up."

"The day she was walking with Paul?"

"Exactly. That was probably part of the appeal—seeing her with another man, getting all jealous and peacocky about it. So he invited her to dinner."

Hugh shrugged. "So he invited her. What's the problem? She's done with that guy. She won't go."

"Shows how well you know your daughter. She's going. One night off a week, she's wasting it on that jerk."

"But that's a terrible idea!"

"Hurrah," said Sheila, "there's something we agree on."

"But why—"

"Come on, Hugh, figure it out. It's basically the same deal you used to offer to your ladies. Pleasant empty calories. He's not for real. She can see him, not see him, sleep with him, not sleep with him, and it just plain doesn't matter."

Pawing at the turf, Barnett said, "But what a waste! Let's just tell her not to go."

Sheila coughed out a mirthless little laugh. "That's a good one. We can't do that. She'll do what she wants. Most we can do, maybe we can have a little influence."

"When's the dinner?" Barnett asked.

"Tuesday. Time and place to be determined."

"I'll be there," Darcy's father said.

"I was hoping you'd say that."

There was a softness, almost a catch in Sheila's voice as she said those words. But she seemed intent on putting aside that tone and getting back to business. "Now, about your lady cellist."

"Yes?"

"I can probably find her. But even if I do, there's one big fat possible problem. Do you know if she already has a soul mate?"

"Excuse me?"

"Soul. Mate. Which part don't you understand?"

"I understand the words. But come on, what's the big deal? People talk about soul mates all the time. Two people both like— what?—hardware stores, Marx Brothers movies, people say they're soul mates. You know, it's just a figure of speech."

"Not around here, it isn't. Up here it has a precise and technical meaning. And it is a big deal. Maybe the biggest deal of all."

Barnett rubbed his chin, looked down at his feet.

"It means," Sheila went on, "that two beings are linked forever. I don't think you can even imagine that. It's not like they're mates until they aren't. They don't slip away and mingle their essence elsewhere. They're joined. Completed. It's like a chemical bond, the mother of all commitments. Get it?"

Her ex-husband fidgeted and fumbled. "And everybody has one?"

"A soul mate? No, not everyone. Not by a long shot."

"But if people were happily married—"

"I guess that's a start," said Sheila. "But remember that line from the vows? *Till death do us part?* Living people misinterpret that. They think it means forever. But think about the words. It's really an escape clause. Death parts them, the vows are kaput, the contract is over.

And let's face it, sometimes, even in a happy marriage, enough is enough. Time to renegotiate. Or just die and move on. Maybe there's something better out there. Maybe your soul mate is someone you haven't even met yet."

"Even after you're dead?"

"Sure. Why not? You think there's only one way these things happen? Look, with the happily married people, if they're truly soul mates, they're ahead of the game. They'll be reunited eventually. Trust me on this. It's like a place is reserved. But people who weren't coupled up, or who spent their lives with the wrong person, they get another shot."

Trying to get his mind around the notion, Barnett said, "So this woman Emma. Even though she was married all those years, up here she could still be…what would you say? Single? Available?"

"If she was married to the wrong man, yes."

Barnett could not help laughing. "I've never thought of dead people as being single."

"There's probably a lot of things you've never thought of. Like death being another word for second chance. But look, we don't have singles bars, we don't have dating websites, we don't have social mixers on Friday nights. Still, beings sometimes manage to get together. If it's meant to be, it'll find a way to happen."

Barnett was suddenly assailed by another thought. "And what about you?"

"What about me, what?"

"Your soul mate."

"I don't seem to have one," Sheila said. If she was wistful about it, it didn't come through in her voice. "Like I said, not everybody does. Sometimes it's better to be alone. On Earth, up here—sometimes it's better. It's fine."

"Maybe you and I are soul mates," said her former husband. "Maybe we're meant to be together after all."

"Please, Hugh, don't make me laugh. After everything that happened?"

"You just said people get a second chance up here."

"Right. But there's such a thing as screwing up the first chance so royally that the second chance just isn't going to happen. Or not with me, at least."

A tone somewhere between persuasion and pleading came into his voice. "But we've cleared the air. We understand things so much better now. What's that French saying? To understand all is to forgive all."

"Very poetic," said Sheila. "And totally self-serving. Besides, you're overlooking one small detail. We're not French."

"And this being alone business. You say it's okay, it's fine. I'm not sure I believe you."

"Believe me, don't believe me. I don't care."

"Can't we even *think* about getting back together?"

"No."

Barnett pawed at the turf. He thought about the prospect of being unattached for all eternity, and the idea terrified him. The fear, in turn, gave rise to a conviction that he hadn't been able to muster in his lifetime. "I'm not giving up on this, Sheila."

"That's very flattering," his dead wife said, as she was already starting to slip from view. "But I'm telling you, you're wasting your time. I'll get back to you about the cellist."

32.

Paul DeFiore was pacing around his loft apartment. This was not something he usually did. When he had something on his mind, he usually mulled it over, slowly and silently, while working in the vineyard or the winery. Questions simmered at the back of his brain while most of his attention was on the task at hand. Often he would find that a question had been answered, a problem solved, less by conscious logic than by the moving of his limbs and the full use of his senses and his skills. Things tended to fall into place as he worked, as long as he didn't force them, as long as he was patient.

But today he wasn't feeling very patient. He was wrestling with a simple but intense dilemma, and he couldn't seem either to sit still or do his work until it was resolved. He was deciding whether to call Darcy that day. Was it too soon to call? Did she want to hear from him at all? He *thought* she did…but the way she'd bolted after their quick kiss was so abrupt, so herky-jerky. He hadn't gotten to ask if he could see her again. She hadn't given him her number or asked for his. She'd simply vanished. The whole episode had been intriguing but also a little bit bizarre.

So what should he do? He paced, he exhaled, and finally he all but dove to his desk and picked up the phone. He called her at the restaurant.

It was just before lunchtime, and when the call was transferred to the kitchen there was a lot of noise on the line. Pans were clanging. Steam was hissing. Paul said hello. There was a brief pause, as if, amid the chaos, Darcy hadn't quite recognized his voice.

"Oh, hi," she said at last. The tone seemed friendly but nothing more.

"I really enjoyed our talk the other day."

"So did I."

He wondered: Did she say that just because she had to, because it was the polite reply? If it was anything more than that, why did she say so little?

"Well," he said, "I won't keep you, but I'm hoping maybe we can have dinner or something one of these evenings. Do you get a night off?"

In the bustling kitchen, Darcy looked down at the tile floor. It registered only hazily that this was a crucial moment, a moment she might look back on either with nostalgia or remorse. Too often, such pivotal moments had a way of cropping up at the worst imaginable times, times when it was impossible to give them the thought and care they called for. She was distracted. She felt hurried. Pressuring herself to answer, she realized she was about to tell a lie. She didn't want to lie; it was less a decision than a faulty reflex, a botched attempt to keep things simple. "Usually Tuesday," she said. "But not this week. I'm filling in for someone."

Happily unaware that he was being lied to, Paul said, "How about next Tuesday, then?"

"Sure. That would be great. But listen, I have to go for now."

They hung up. Paul felt terrific. He had a date a week from Tuesday. He didn't mind the delay. He sort of savored the suspense.

Darcy felt dreadful, queasy, as if she'd bitten into something rotten. Lies were very odd things. Over time, maybe, they hurt the person being lied to, but the person doing the lying was stung and diminished right away. Why had she done it? She hardly knew Paul; she didn't owe him any explanations. She could have simply said she had other plans, and left it at that. She was a single woman; she was entitled to see Charles or anybody else. Why was this new man making that seem like a problem? Squirming out from under her own chagrin, she began somehow to blame Paul for the fact that she had been dishonest. The lie now stood between them; it would make it difficult for her to look Paul in the eye.

Hugh Barnett heard fiddle music.

To his unpracticed ear, the piece sounded familiar though he couldn't quite place it. The music was sinuous and sly. Its melody traveled a certain distance, then, like a person who'd forgotten his hat, it doubled back, retracing a tune that had lingered only as an echo. Even an amateur could tell that there was genius in the music, less so in the playing. Here and there a note, sagging like an exhausted runner, dragged itself to its appointed pitch; now and then a phrase seemed shapeless, draped in a sack rather than a sheath.

Even so, the music was intriguing, and Barnett moved in its direction. He found Manny Klein playing in front of a green-and-white striped tent. If he'd had an open violin case at his feet, he would have looked exactly like a superannuated music student playing on the street, soliciting bills and change. He acknowledged his friend with the smallest of nods and continued to the end of the movement.

When the music stopped, Barnett applauded in a lukewarm sort of way. "Nice. What was it?"

"What was it? It was the same Bach fugue you heard me play me before. I'm working on a new rendition. What did you think?"

Barnett shuffled his feet uncomfortably. "I'm no expert."

"Come on," said Manny. "Tell me. You won't hurt my feelings."

"Okay. I liked the other way better."

To his surprise, the old fiddler seemed delighted with the assessment. "That's exactly what I was hoping you would say."

"Really? I don't get it."

Manny gestured with the violin. "The other way *was* better. It was beautiful, it was gorgeous. Only problem is that it wasn't really me that was playing it. Something weird was going on. I'd go through the motions and the music just happened. Hard to explain. It was like a dead person's version of a lip-sync. Too slick. Sort of phony. This whole perfection business—it's nice, I guess, but it just isn't me. If I played that way for Emma, she'd know I was bullshitting, she'd see through it in about ten seconds. So I'm trying to play the way I used to. Have you seen your wife?"

"Yeah, I have."

Manny's eyes bulged. He leaned far forward over his toes. "And?"

"She's looking for Emma."

"Looking?"

"That's all I know. If she'll find her, how long it might take, I really have no idea."

"You're killing me with this."

"Sorry, Manny. I'm doing the best I can."

"When, if. You have no idea at all?"

"If it's meant to be, it'll happen. That's what she said. Come on, we have forever. Try to be patient."

"Patient," Manny said. Then he shrugged. "I'll tell you something about patient. It's another way of saying helpless. Have you ever heard, in the entire history of the universe, of anybody being patient if they have a choice?"

Not waiting for an answer, he tucked the fiddle underneath his chin and resumed his efforts at playing imperfectly.

33.

Beyond the Second Membrane, people were free to choose the degree of privacy that suited them most comfortably. They could be gregarious or reclusive, available to everyone or no one.

Emma Winthrop had chosen a quite private, though not hermetic, existence. It wasn't that she didn't enjoy people; some of her happiest memories revolved around the playing of chamber music, with its fierce attention to one's partners, its intimate twining and exchanging of emotions and ideas.

Still, in her earthly tenure, she'd been much imposed upon; she'd surrendered, more or less willingly, many of her own prerogatives. Most of her professional life had been spent as an orchestra player; her musical voice had been subsumed into a grand but impersonal edifice of sound, and bent to the will of sometimes tyrannical conductors. Add to that a half-century of marriage to a demanding and rather self-centered husband, and it was understandable that Emma had chosen largely to be left alone with her cello and her thoughts.

This made her a bit difficult to find.

But time was not an issue, and discouragement did not penetrate beyond the Second Membrane. Sheila Barnett patiently wafted from neighborhood to neighborhood in search of her.

In that abstract sphere, beings had the option of taking up no space at all, or of crafting a space that best suited their temperament and their whim. Emma Winthrop had conjured a space around herself that was very much like a rehearsal room at a conservatory. Radically austere, it featured a few simple chairs and a music stand. There was a suggestion of cozy, enveloping walls, though the walls were not opaque. There was the semblance of a doorway though there was no need of a door.

Sheila stood in that doorway now; Emma did not immediately notice her. She was playing Brahms and was completely immersed in the soaring and swooping music. At the end of the movement, Sheila applauded.

Emma, for the first time, looked up. It had been a long while since she'd heard applause. Hearing it now was not unpleasant, though it mostly struck her that the clapping of hands to show approval was a peculiar and archaic custom, and faintly ridiculous at that. Why did people do it? For that matter, why did so many people need so badly to hear it? Why did people work so hard, dedicate their lives, stake their self-esteem on getting other people to smack their palms together like excited chimpanzees?

"That was beautiful," Sheila said.

"Thank you."

"Do you mind if I come in?"

Surprised but not displeased to have a visitor, Emma put the cello aside and waved her in with the bow.

Sheila introduced herself and sat down in a folding chair. "This is really nice," she said. "Sort of Quaker. So nice and plain."

"Rooms like this are where I was always most at ease. Small, quiet. Nothing extra. In concert halls I felt like I was disappearing. What's your place like?"

Sheila laughed. "Me? I decided I didn't want a place. I used to spend way too much time indoors, cooped up. Offices. Studios. I worked in television news. Endless hours. Plus I always hated housework and was pretty lousy at it. Who needs it? I'm happier just wafting."

"Ah, a nomad."

"Nomad. Free spirit. Bag lady. Depends what kind of spin you want to put on it."

There was a silence. It was a friendly silence, but, even so, it soon grew slightly awkward.

Sheila said, "I guess you're wondering why I stopped by."

"Well, actually, yes, I was."

"I feel a little funny launching in. I don't want to complicate anything for you."

Emma gestured around the all but empty room. "I doubt that'll be a problem. I've kept things pretty basic."

"Well, okay then. Okay. I'm here on behalf of a friend. And I wanted to ask you if you've chosen someone yet."

"Chosen?" Emma felt her face flush and grow warm. It had been a long time since she'd felt that. "You mean a mate? No, I haven't."

"But you were married for a long time, yes?"

"I was. To a good man, though a difficult one. I'm pretty sure I loved him. But I'm just as happy being rid of him. Is that terrible to say?"

"Honey, I've said way worse things about my ex. But then, he wasn't much good for Earth *or* eternity. But, do you mind going solo up here? Are you ever lonely?"

Emma toyed with the bow, ran fingertips along its coarse fibers. "Sometimes. A little. Not much. I used to imagine that the dead must be very lonely. You know, shut up in a box or stuck in an urn somewhere. Eventually demoted from the mantelpiece to the attic. Away from everybody. But it's kind of a relief. You know what I mean?"

"Do I ever," Sheila said. She paused, and Emma found herself leaning forward in her simple chair. "Well," her visitor said at last, "I feel a little silly, playing matchmaker to dead people. But if you're interested, there's someone who'd like to see you again. I think maybe you know who it is."

Emma nodded slightly, then looked down. She touched her silver hair and ran her fingertips across her forehead and along her cheeks; she could feel the creases in her skin and the crinkles at the corners of her eyes. "But, my God, I'm an old woman."

"Not to him, you're not. To him, you're twenty-five and very beautiful."

"Manny." Saying his name out loud made her shake her head and smile. "Have you met him?"

Sheila said that she had not.

"He's a character. He's funny."

"And he's still carrying a torch for you."

Emma blushed. "I think you're probably exaggerating."

"Did you know he never married?"

"That's a shame. He would have made a good husband for someone."

"How about a soul mate?"

Emma gave a nervous laugh.

"He's available. You're available…"

"But this is crazy. This is way too sudden."

"So take your time. No pressure. None at all. He waited his whole life, he can wait a while longer."

At that, Emma grew a shade less agitated and more confiding. "You know," she said, "I've thought about him. A lot. When I was alive. Since I've been up here. But I just don't know if I should trust what I remember. Maybe I'm making it seem better than it was. Maybe it wasn't even Manny that seemed so wonderful, maybe it was just being young. How can I tell? I haven't seen him in forever."

"Would you like to see him?" Sheila asked.

Emma pursed her lips but didn't answer.

"Well," said her visitor, "if you decide you want to, just show up. I promise he'll still be waiting."

34.

On his second call to Darcy, Charles McPherson, a veteran seducer and a pretty decent cook, had suggested that they have dinner at his house in Montecito. What could be nicer for a restaurant pro than to have a simple but elegant home-cooked meal presented to her on her one night off?

It was a tempting offer but Darcy saw through it. She knew that house. She remembered the soft blue light that lay like a quilt above the swimming pool, the bank of jasmine that grew behind the hot tub. She remembered where the bedroom was; she knew about the terry-cloth robes that hung behind the bathroom door. Going to that house would rig the odds, would greatly increase the chances that she would end up back in bed with Charles.

She was hoping that wouldn't happen. But of course she was teasing herself that it might. It was a convoluted little game she was playing entirely in her mind. At moments she recognized it as a game, a contrivance, an artificial test; at other moments, she pretended it was all in earnest, as though Charles mattered to her one way or the other. At other moments again, fleeting and blurred, she vaguely understood that the whole ill-advised experiment had almost nothing to do with Charles and was all about Paul.

In any case, she'd held her ground about not going to the house in Montecito, and Charles had moved on to Plan B. He had a beautiful car, a low-slung two-seater, powerful and intimate. Why didn't they take a nice ride out to the wine country? A leisurely drive at sunset, an unhurried meal with a good bottle or two, a meander back home by the light of the moon?

Wine country? Paul's part of the world? That would make things a little riskier, a little edgier; more reckless, maybe, but also more substantial. By the perverse but airtight logic of the game she was playing, ramping up the risk, like surviving a round Russian roulette, might even be a kind of affirmation; if she passed that danger, then maybe she could face the bigger risk of getting serious and opening her heart to Paul.

Besides, wine country stretched for many miles, through several towns, with dozens of restaurants. It wasn't *that* dangerous to go there. She said it sounded perfect. Charles made a reservation for a quiet table.

At the Café in Los Olivos, Paul and Josh were comparing a few different styles of Syrah. One wine, grown in the coolest part of the valley, tasted of raspberries and pepper. Another, from a vineyard barely two miles away but blocked from the ocean breeze, was all blueberry and plum. Yet another, dosed with just a tiny percentage of Viognier, took on a completely different violet perfume.

As ever, the two friends talked as they sniffed and swirled. At some point Josh asked Paul how things were going with the chef.

He put his glass down before he answered. He toyed with the stem of it and stared at his fingertips. Finally he said, "I don't quite know what to make of it, but I think I'm sort of smitten."

"Smitten?" said Josh. "Wow. And all you've done is take a walk?"

"Pretty much. A walk on the beach. One little hug. A quick kiss goodbye."

Josh cut straight to the chase. "On the lips?"

"Well, that's the thing. I'm not quite sure."

"How can you not be sure if a kiss is on the lips?"

"It was sort of—"

"A palate like yours, you don't know where your lips are?"

"It was, like, right on the edge. It might've been an accident."

"It was not an accident."

Paul sipped some wine. "Anyway, there's something about her. The way she meets your eyes. Most people, you look at them, right away there's a feeling that they're hiding something. You know what I mean? I'm not saying hiding anything awful. Just not letting you see the whole picture. Just trying to make it seem like life is easy, everything is fine and dandy. Darcy's not like that. She lets things show."

"Like what kind of things?"

Paul tilted a glass, examined the wine's depth of color. "Well, like her parents were divorced—"

"So were everybody's, except yours."

"—and her father was a runaround, and she knew that from when she was a kid, and that's something she's had to deal with."

"So, not to put too fine a point on it, she thinks all men are bastards?"

"She sort of thinks that, I guess. But she's trying *not* to think it. That's part of what you see in her eyes."

Josh nipped at one of the Syrahs, then pushed it aside. "Way too jammy for me. What would it go with, waffles? You're making me a little nervous."

"I'm making myself a little nervous," Paul admitted.

"No one asked my opinion, but this sounds a little too much like your basic rescuer scenario."

"You think I haven't thought of that? But look, it's not like she's miserably unhappy and I'm supposed to be the white knight that fixes everything. She's trying to figure things out for herself. She just needs someone not to be a total jerk while she works on it."

"Think you can manage it?"

"Very funny."

"But okay, I get it. She works through her crap, then it's your turn to be scared shitless."

"Why would I be—?"

"Come on," Josh said, "it's so obvious. Darcy's parents had a lousy marriage, so her fear is that love affairs are doomed to crash and burn. Your parents were more that 1930s movie, my-one-and-only kind of deal, so your fear is that, if something gets even a little bit serious, that's it, the die is cast, you're locked in till you croak."

"That isn't what I think."

"I didn't say it's what you think. I said it's what you fear. It's really kind of funny. Your fear, her fear, they're really sort of opposites. If there were just some way that they could average out…"

He let the thought tail off as he slid down from his barstool and settled his tab. Paul did the same, and they zig-zagged through the dining room that was just starting to fill up.

Out on the street, the light was soft and purple; there was a coppery gleam on the storefronts. Springtime was advancing; the days were getting longer, the dusks more sensuous and velvety. There seemed to be almost a precise moment when the parched warmth of the afternoon gave way to the moist coolness of the evening, when the hills beyond the village lost their crisp edges and softened in haze.

The street was very quiet--just a few people strolling here and there, the occasional car driving around the flagpole--and Paul took no particular notice when a navy-blue Porsche came purring down the road and pivoted into a parking space a few doors down from where he and Josh were walking. It registered only dimly when a trim and tidy man emerged from the driver's side door. Then a woman appeared across from him. She had thick, unruly russet hair. Bundles of it broke free and tumbled down across her forehead; she swept them back again with quick, unconscious motions.

Paul grabbed Josh by the arm and pulled him quickly around a corner.

Surprised at the yank, he said, "What's up?"

Paul shook his head, stared down at the sidewalk, then gestured backwards with his chin and said in a choked whisper, "That was her. Darcy. With someone else."

"You're sure?"

Paul nodded. "She told me she was working tonight."

"Fuck. Sorry."

Paul took a big long breath then blew it out again.

His friend patted him on the shoulder as they continued walking rather aimlessly down the side street. "Look at the bright side. Seems you're off the hook. Better to know sooner than later, right?"

35.

"That was bad," said Hugh Barnett, turning away from the viewing device with the hammered aluminum smiley-face.

"Really bad," his former wife agreed.

"Can't we undo it? Rewind the tape? Change the timing or something?"

"Sorry, Hugh, it doesn't work that way."

Exasperated, he said, "I don't see why she went there in the first place."

"You don't? The thing with Paul, she's giving it every chance to fail, so that if it doesn't she can believe it's meant to be."

Barnett frowned and wagged his head. "Except it looks like she's already blown it."

"We don't know that for sure."

"Come on. He's really pissed."

"People forgive."

"Oh, do they? According to you, of all people? She really hurt his feelings."

"Hurt feelings," Sheila said, "that's life. Nobody dies of hurt feelings. In the meantime, all we can do is try not to let things get any worse. You ready to go?"

In Earth terms, it took them no time at all to travel to the funky turquoise diving board. It cost Barnett only a fleeting spasm of anxiety to climb the steps, walk the plank, and take the plunge. The Membrane curdled him like a failed emulsion and bound him back together on the other side.

His ears crackling with a faint static, he arrived in downtown Los Olivos. By a weatherman's long habit, he checked the western horizon. Mare's tail clouds were thickening into a mackerel sky; the day's last light, mauve and inky gray, filtered through the scales. The breeze had stalled; humidity was rising. Perfect conditions for a major change in the weather. Low pressure moving onshore. Storms. High winds. Drama. Yeah, right. He'd made that prediction hundreds of times, and nearly always been wrong.

He slipped into the Cafe dining room to find Darcy fidgeting with a corner of her napkin as Charles McPherson was perusing the wine list.

He ordered a bottle of champagne, to be followed by a pricey Pinot Noir from the Santa Rita Hills. As they clinked glasses, Charles took the opportunity to send Darcy a soulful gray-eyed glance that she did not return in kind. "It's wonderful to see you," he said. "I've really missed you. To be honest, more than I expected to."

She took that with a grain of salt and studied her host over the rim of her glass. He was a good-looking man, square-jawed and ruddy, though prosperity and indulgence were beginning to make him a little thick beneath the chin and just slightly puffy around the eyes.

"Why did we even break up?" he went on. "Did we even have a decent reason?"

"*I* did. You were screwing everything that walked."

Charles didn't deny it. Nor could he entirely hide a look of goofy pride that Darcy's father, hovering above their table, recognized with a guilty wince.

"I was in a pretty wild phase," he said. "I admit it. It was like this spasm of relief once the divorce was over with. But I've settled down a lot. Really."

Darcy said nothing; it was all the same to her if Charles had settled down or not. He refilled their glasses. The waiter came over to take their order. Salmon with a sorrel sauce for her, calf's liver finished with Calvados for him.

Picking up the thread, he said, "Actually, you're the one who seems to be getting around these days."

"Meaning?"

"That guy you were all hunkered down with at the beach."

"Hunkered down? We were having a conversation."

"Looked pretty intense."

"It was."

"So who is he?"

"None of your business."

Hugh smiled secretly. He was impressed with Darcy's firmness and composure. She seemed so relaxed; then again, why shouldn't she be? Seeing Charles was not an adventure but a retreat.

Refilling their champagne flutes, he said, "I thought he looked a little rustic for you."

"Rustic?"

"The blue jeans. The plaid shirt. Just a little...rustic. I picture you with someone more sophisticated."

Ah, thought Hugh Barnett, the old running-down-the-competition trick. He'd used that one himself. Sometimes it worked; sometimes it backfired.

Darcy said, "Rustic. Hm. Paul has a master's from Davis and has worked work in Tuscany and Burgundy. That's your idea of rustic?"

"Paul?"

"Paul DeFiore." Darcy felt an element of bracing defiance in saying his name. In a somewhat twisted way it was an act of loyalty. "He grows grapes and makes wine."

"Ah. A man of the soil. The whole dirt-under-the-fingernails kind of thing. You sleeping with him yet?"

"None of your business."

The food arrived. Plates were carefully turned to best advantage, cutlery double-checked. Casually but masterfully, Charles said to the waiter, "We'll take the Pinot now." Then, to Darcy, he continued, "Come on. We're old friends, worldly people. Can't we have a candid conversation?"

"Not about that. No."

"Maybe you'll tell me later," he teased. "Bon appétit."

They ate. Darcy approved of the salmon. It was crispy on top and translucent at the center; the sorrel sauce was bitingly tart.

Charles sipped wine, then fastidiously wiped his lips with his napkin. "You know," he said, "I'm happy for you, I really am, that you've gotten interested in someone else. I haven't been that lucky."

She didn't believe him, but what did it matter? "So you've just been sitting home and pining for me?"

"Not exactly, no. But I've been realizing that, what we had together, it's not so easy to find."

Darcy drank more of the Pinot and noticed all at once that she was getting tipsy. It was an odd sort of tipsiness, in that it made some things seem more blurry and others seem more clear. What was clearer was that she really wished she wasn't sitting there with Charles. What was blurrier was why she'd agreed to do this in the first place and how the evening would end up. Contending emotions flickered past and made her suddenly irritable. Rather feistily, she said, "Oh? And what was it, exactly, that we had together?"

Uncharacteristically, Charles seemed thrown by the directness of the question.

"Some nice meals," Darcy went on. "A few openings and benefits where you seemed very pleased to have a younger woman on your arm. Some pleasant lovemaking, at your convenience. And some talk about really spending time together, getting closer, which somehow never happened. That's what I remember."

Charles fingered the base of his wineglass and looked extremely contrite. Hugh Barnett recognized the tactic; contrition could be very disarming. "I'm sorry if you see it that way. I didn't realize you were still angry with me."

Darcy drank more wine, which at that moment might not have been the best idea. Or maybe it was. Perhaps, as in a fever dream, maximum confusion was a prelude to clarity. Finally she said, "I'm not angry with you. I'm angry with myself. I shouldn't have come here tonight."

"Then why did you?"

She said nothing, but in her mind a powerful if not exactly rational answer was taking shape. She'd come because she was terribly afraid she was falling in love with that rustic guy, with Paul.

Completely misreading her silence, Charles said, "Maybe it's because you still enjoy my company. Because we understand each other."

There was such a vast gulf between his words and Darcy's thoughts that she could find nothing to say in return.

Undaunted, he purred, "Look, why don't we spend the night together? For old times' sake. I think it would be wonderful. If it doesn't feel right to you, we part as friends in the morning. What's the harm?"

She tipped her chin downward and stared at her hands. Was she wavering? She was disappointed with herself for being there; already feeling diminished, she could easily say yes to Charles, drink more wine, spend the night, and feel diminished further. What's the harm? What the hell?

Her father watched her, fending off a kind of guilty panic, searching for words, struggling for focus. He compressed himself into an urgent thought. *Wait! My sweet daughter, wait. There is harm. Harm to your heart. Harm to your chances for happiness. Wasting time on a guy like this--you think you're protecting yourself from hurt, from disappointment? You're doing just the opposite. You're guaranteeing disappointment. Believe me, I know. Haven't you noticed that Charles is an awful lot like your old man? Maybe you're just too close to see it. Maybe it's so obvious you look right past it. But come on. There's nothing here for you. Nothing good, at least. You know that, deep down. You deserve better; you know that, too. Move on. You have to believe you're ready to move on.*

Darcy raised her eyes. Charles was still looking at her, waiting for an answer. She studied him a moment—the handsome jaw, the mischievous gaze. Slowly, gently, she shook her head. She even smiled. She no longer felt feisty; she was suddenly just a little tired, fatigued from the wine and a sense of relief she hadn't realized she'd feel. "Charles," she said, "I'm sorry if I've been a tease. I haven't meant to be, I promise. But I'm not going to sleep with you again. It would just be a really bad idea."

He got the news and blinked. "Ah," was all he said. She couldn't tell if he was surprised or not surprised. If he was crushed, it didn't show. His smile collapsed just briefly but soon returned, albeit dialed down a notch.

An awkward moment passed. Darcy sat with her hands in her lap. Charles fidgeted with a fork. At last he said, "Dessert?"

Maybe he was being a good sport. Maybe he was taking one last shot at seduction. To Darcy it didn't matter one way or the other. "Thanks but no," she said. "I'd like it if you'd take me home now."

36.

Emma Winthrop could hardly believe what she was doing: She was trying on clothes.

Though it should be understood that, in her ethereal neighborhood, clothing was made not of fabric but of memories, and attached not with buttons or clasps, but by imagination. So Emma recalled the colors and styles she'd been wearing in the cherished moments when she'd felt most vibrantly alive, most fully herself. She tried on party dresses from the 1940s and shirtwaists from the '50s. She tried on concert gowns and pantsuits. She modeled sweaters that she had favored as an ingénue, and silk jackets that more befitted a mature, accomplished woman. She was still trying to decide if she would risk her equanimity by meeting with her old flame, Manny; or more likely she had already decided but couldn't quite admit it yet. This worrying about what to wear was both part of the dilemma and a welcome distraction from it.

There were certain nagging questions for which she had no answers. If she met with Manny, what age would each of them appear to be? Did their love affair have its own private clock that had stopped when they parted? Or had time ignored the event and just kept barreling along, rendering them, by now, ancient strangers? A lifetime later, would she and Manny even recognize each other?

She wondered if Manny would still be funny; she wondered if she could knock the rust off her own readiness to laugh. If she found that, after all this time—after marriage, after motherhood—she was still in love with Manny, then what? Could passion be rekindled without heartbeats, without a racing pulse? If desire outlived bodies, how did it fulfill itself?

On the other hand, what if a meeting with Manny turned out to be a fiasco, a mockery of her anticipation? What if seeing him again was like revisiting a beloved childhood place, only to find it far less magical and grand than one remembered?

Since leaving Earth, Emma Winthrop had hardly ever felt lonely. She had her music and the very occasional visitor. She asked for and expected nothing more. But suddenly there seemed to be the chance of a companion; this time, the right companion. There was excitement in the possibility, but also danger. A chosen and accepted solitude was a different thing from loneliness. Loneliness was the hollow place, the vacant outline, left behind by a hope that had gone away. Emma was still not quite sure if she should take a chance on hoping.

Hugh Barnett, yanked back once again to the enormous rolling lawn, was all wound up from his adventure in the restaurant. "I helped," he said. "I think I timed it just right and I helped."

Sheila was near him but said nothing. Her glow was slightly dim just then, its tint a little somber, but he was too enthused to notice.

"It was a little strange," he went on, "a little difficult. The way I helped, I pretty much had to make myself the bad guy."

Sheila said, "If the shoe fits…"

"Okay, okay. I don't mind. The truth hurts me a little less these days. That's a good thing, right?" He looked at his ex, waiting for an answer. Only then did he realize how subdued she seemed. "Something wrong?"

"Wrong? Not exactly. Just necessary. There's something I have to tell you. Your chances to go back, they're just about used up."

This should not have come as a shock. It was as inevitable as death itself, and Barnett had been warned that it would happen at some point. Still, the news, coming right on the heels of a victory, struck him as an abrupt and highly personal affront, as though he'd been singled out for what was in fact a universal sorrow. "But why now?"

"Forget about why. There is no why. Or none that I know of."

"But who decides when--?"

"Does there have to be a Someone? I've been here a while and I still have no idea."

"But I've been doing good things."

The protest hung there for a moment, then was swallowed up by the surrounding silence. In the quiet, Barnett tried to reconcile himself to this looming new loss, his final banishment. It felt no easier than the first time he'd been culled from the world. In some ways it felt harder. At his earthly death, there were a few people, at least, to mark his passing, to share his bereavement. This new loss was a secret that no one still in the world would even suspect.

After a pause, his ex-wife said, "You have one more visit, Hugh. Make it count. Finish what you need to do. After that, you can rest."

He nodded. He stared down at the lawn. Then he said, "Do you remember, a while ago, I asked if you went back when you could?"

"I remember. And I didn't answer."

"Why not?"

"You didn't need to know back then. It wouldn't have helped you to know."

"Can you tell me now?"

Sheila looked away a moment before she spoke. "I went back. Of course I went back. Who wouldn't go back if they still had a child on Earth?"

"So what did you do?"

"I went to Darcy and asked her to forgive me."

This took Barnett by surprise. "Forgive you? For what? You were a wonderful mother. You were wonderful to Darcy."

"I left her. I died."

"Sure. Okay. But it's not like it was your fault."

A little wearily, Sheila shook her head. "Not everything that needs forgiving is someone's fault. Some things just need forgiving. She was twenty, and I left. I left her with too much to figure out on her own, too much I'd never got around to explaining. She was angry with me for dying too soon, and I don't blame her."

Barnett started to speak but found no words.

"Besides," she went on, "it wasn't just that I died. It was the times I'd been gloomy, the times I'd stained her life with my own bitterness and disappointments."

"Wait a second," he cut in. "Those things were my fault, not yours."

Sheila managed a quick, soft laugh. "Sorry, Hugh, you can't have *all* the blame. They were my fault too. There were things I should have risen above, for her sake. I didn't have the strength. I needed to apologize for that, to tell her that I'd done my best. And I needed to let her know that, after all the crummy stuff, things had really turned out okay, that I was happy now, and she would be happy, too."

"So you told her that? She got it?"

"I tried to tell her. I hope she got it. How can you ever be sure?"

37.

Paul DeFiore did hard physical work, mostly in the breeze and sunshine. His body was healthy, his conscience was clear, and he usually slept soundly and long.

That night he did not. He tossed and turned; he flipped his pillow and tossed some more beneath the twisted sheet. He was trying to figure out why Darcy had lied to him. If she had another boyfriend, fair enough; she was an attractive young woman--why wouldn't she have another boyfriend? But if she was involved with someone, why would she have kissed him on the corner of the mouth? Why would she have agreed to have dinner? Maybe she was flat out untrustworthy; maybe she was even a little crazy. Maybe Josh was right. Maybe Darcy was irretrievably damaged goods. Not her fault, but what did that matter? Happiness was possible or it wasn't, and the gallant but stupid impulse to play the rescuer could only lead to more of these wasted nights.

Morning came. None of Paul's questions had been answered, but, by default, he'd come to a decision. He wasn't thrilled with the decision but he felt that it was right and necessary. He got up, showered, and, with his eyes itching and skin prickly from fatigue, he jumped into his truck for the ride to Santa Barbara. He wanted to be standing in front of Santa Bistro when Darcy arrived for work.

It was around ten-thirty when she got downtown and pulled into a city lot around the corner from the restaurant.

She felt light this morning, even buoyant. She'd already had a run on the beach; her muscles were taut and her mind was clear of last night's wine and last night's doubts. Seeing Charles, seeing through Charles—it had turned out to be a worthwhile exercise after all. She'd passed a test that no one but herself even suspected was a test, avoided a trap that she herself had set. She now knew what she didn't want and wouldn't settle for, and that made everything seem so much simpler.

Walking quickly, she came around the corner and saw Paul waiting in the middle of the block. For one brief moment she was thrilled to see him, but in the next she was assailed by the suspicion—no, the certainty—that his being there could not be good. She slowed her pace. Her posture stayed the same, but inside something had sagged.

When they were close enough to speak, he said hello.

"Hi," she said. There was already something tentative and wary in the single syllable.

He looked at her. He'd more or less rehearsed what he would say, but seeing her now—the green eyes with the surprising hazel flecks, the brave shoulders that always seemed tilted toward a headwind—he got flustered. Rubbing his chin, stammering a bit, he said, "I'm sorry to just show up like this. But listen, our dinner, I need to cancel. I just don't think it's a good idea."

"Oh." She met his gaze for just an instant, then looked down at the sidewalk.

"I saw you in Los Olivos last night." He hadn't meant to say this but found he couldn't help it.

She nodded just slightly, as if she wasn't really so surprised. Going to his neighborhood, after all, had been part of the gamble, part of the self-set trap. She'd thought she'd avoided the snares, outsmarted the maze; apparently she hadn't. Well, that was how things went. She'd given herself an out, and just when she decided she didn't really want the exit, there it was, yawning open, pulling her through. An old story for Darcy—except this time there was something different about it. She felt no relief, only loss. She felt that she couldn't just shrug and move on. "I'm sorry," she said. "I can explain."

Paul raised a wine-stained hand to fend her off. "You don't have to. It's probably better if you don't."

"But—"

"I really like you, Darcy. But I don't like games. I'm not good at them and I don't have time for them. I need to call this off. I'm sorry."

She pressed her lips together, then looked past Paul and down the street. It was like any other morning. People shopping, going out for coffee, trying to navigate their lives without running up on rocks or shoals. More to herself than Paul, she said, "I really messed this up."

He could find nothing to say to that. He just gave a sheepish shrug. For a moment they stood very still on the sidewalk, a couple of feet apart. There would have been comfort in a parting hug; but there would have been fresh risk as well, and neither of them took the chance. They mumbled their mutual apologies once again, and she slipped past him into the restaurant.

38.

For Hugh Barnett, peering through the viewer behind the low white picket fence had ceased to be mere sightseeing and had become a sacred mission. He had just one more chance to visit with his daughter. If there was anguish in the certainty of that, there was also opportunity. Much depended on seizing the proper moment.

So he studied Darcy all through the day and evening. At work, even though her brief conversation with Paul was playing and replaying in her mind, she showed almost nothing of her upset. She prepped; she cooked; she went about her business. She was a grown-up with a job to do.

It wasn't until she was driving home, around eleven, that her composure started breaking down. Driving the freeway that was pinched between the ocean and the hills, she finally exhaled and unclenched. She didn't cry, but her eyes throbbed with a congestion of tears that wouldn't fall. She'd blown it with Paul. She'd thrown away something good. Why? Because, after almost thirty years of life, it had taken her exactly one evening too long to see things clearly? The way things had played out—was it just plain bad luck? She was way too tough on herself to believe that. She'd arranged the failure, set up her escape. As usual. That's what she was, an escape artist. Great. She'd escaped yet again.

At home in her apartment, she poured herself a glass of wine, then raised a window blind and sat looking out at the night.

Motionless and untiring on the giant lawn, her father watched over her and strained to hear her thoughts. What he heard was a refrain that kept going round and round. Yearning and mistrust and disappointment. Disappointment and yearning and mistrust. It was a maddening and obsessive sequence; it kept repeating like the relentless toots and piping of a garish carousel. It was a pattern that became a cage.

Patterns were powerful; that, the weatherman understood. But sometimes patterns could be broken. Sometimes they were swept away.

Sometimes wild cleansing storms surged through and created a rare chance to start over.

Barnett peered past Darcy's shoulder and through her window. The clouds he'd noticed the night before—fish-scale clouds--had now fused at the edges, had thickened and merged into a fat and pillowy layer. Updrafts were stretching the layer skyward, warping it into a purple billow that was miles tall. Inside this towering cloud, vapor would be swirling; droplets, thwarted in their fall, would be swept upward once again, growing, freezing, turning crystalline. The crystals would slam and scrape together, making tiny sparks that would gather into cataclysmic charges.

Barnett had been wrong in his predictions a hundred times, a thousand times before. No matter. He now believed with all his heart that the weather was about to change. Conditions were exactly right for thunderstorms and hail, for a majestic and cathartic cloudburst that would rip the old pattern to tatters, that would scour the sky with lightning, spice the air with the blue smell of electricity, and make it seem, at least for a day, that everything was clean and new again.

39.

Manny Klein felt a sudden and overwhelming desire for a cup of tea.

He could not have said where this instant craving came from; he hadn't felt it the moment before. But it was irresistible. With his violin and bow held loosely at his side, he walked the lawn until he reached one of the green-and-white-striped tents.

Pulling back the flap, he slipped inside and found an old-fashioned teapot on a table with a linen cloth. Two cups had been laid out. Manny blinked to make sure he'd counted right. The omens seemed to be piling up in a way that was all but unbearable. Why the tea craving? Why two cups? What else could it possibly be? He didn't want to think too much about it. He didn't want to be wrong.

For what seemed like a long time, no one joined him in the tent. He fidgeted. He ran his fingertips along the teapot's curving spout. He looked around the tent for posts or wires, trying without success to figure out how it was supported. He drank tea.

At length he picked up his fiddle. He gave no thought to what he would play; he just started playing. A few notes in, he realized he was playing something that he and Emma had often practiced together. It was Brahms, one of those passages in a slow but pulsing, gypsy kind of rhythm, the voices now twining like interlaced fingers, now chasing one another in languorous pursuit. In his mind, he heard the missing parts, the viola and the piano. Then he realized that, from somewhere outside the tent, he was hearing Emma's cello, answering his phrases, winding over and around his melody. He believed he could have recognized her tone, its warmth and sheen, in a chorus of a thousand players.

In the next moment she was standing in the doorway.

To Manny, she looked as she had looked in 1950. Her dark brown hair was thick and short; it ended in a bouncy curl exactly halfway down her ears. She smiled, but even so her eyes turned downward at their outside corners. She wore a dress with buttons to the waist and a flowing skirt; it had an off-white background and a pattern like the moviehouse candy, Spearmint Leaves.

To Emma, Manny was once again a lean but rumpled conservatory student, his hair and brows wiry and extravagant, his black eyes humorous and kind, his eager posture defined by the violinist's forward-craning neck.

Sitting there at the table with the linen cloth, Manny for a time could neither rise nor speak. Words, he felt, would surely push tears before them. Motion might break the spell, shatter the moment. So he simply gazed at the woman who had been the love of his life, and whom, on Earth, he had met too soon. His eyes burned; his lip quivered. Finally, he managed the only sentence he thought he could say without dissolving entirely. "Would you like a cup of tea?"

40.

Barnett kept his vigil far into the night, until his daughter was in her deepest sleep. Then, alone, he traveled to the funky turquoise diving board. He didn't need an escort this time; he didn't require any coaxing. He was utterly determined.

But when he reached the board that spanned the seam between worlds, he found another man there ahead of him, laboring up the metal steps.

To Barnett, this was not only a surprise but an affront. He'd come to think of this particular diving board as entirely his own. Other people used it, too? Obsessed with his mission, he resented having to wait his turn. Impatiently, he stared at the other man's back, silently urging him along. But the newcomer climbed slowly. His legs were thick and solid, his back was broad but bent, as though from a lifetime of crouching and lifting. His slowness, Barnett gradually understood, was partly based on fear, as his own delays had been. Sensing this, he felt a compassion that tempered his impatience, but only up to a point. He tried not to fidget as he waited for the other man to jump. Vaguely, it occurred to him to wonder why this other traveler was visible to him. During his time on the giant lawn, he'd seen nobody but Sheila and Manny; why had this stranger emerged from the mass of invisible beings and taken on human form?

At last the stranger jumped. He streaked downward for some fraction of a second. The board recoiled with a rattle and a squeak. Then it was as if he'd never been there.

Making up lost time, Barnett quickly seized the handrails, scampered up the steps, and strode decisively to the end of the board. He drew in a big sharp breath, as if in anticipation of being underwater. He leaped into space and plummeted Earthward, passing through the Membrane with an ease commensurate to his purity of purpose.

In the sky above the California coast, he fell into the turbulent and still expanding cloud. Updrafts stalled his descent, creating an illusory heaviness, as when a fast down elevator slammed on the brakes.

Spiraling currents caught him in their dizzying gyre and tossed him skyward once again. Flying, spinning, he wove among ice crystals that switched on and off like a million tiny bulbs as the electricity between them arced and crackled.

Below, the world was sleeping, and after the tumult of the cloud, Darcy's apartment seemed as hushed and still as a cathedral. In recent years, Barnett had seldom visited his daughter at home; that had been part of the distance between them. On the rare occasions when they got together, it was usually on neutral ground—a beach, a restaurant. The everyday particulars of their separate lives remained unshared. Now, visiting for the final time, he drank in details as if the littlest of them—the fringe on a rug, a dent in a throw pillow—were clues to some great riddle. There was just so much he would never know.

At length he drifted into his daughter's bedroom to watch her sleep. She slept on her side, her knees drawn up. One arm was underneath the covers, and the other extended out, the hand relaxed, the fingers at rest. Her hair was splayed across the pillow.

Sleeping, she looked very young, still a child almost, and Barnett discovered that somewhere deep inside himself he was weeping. He was weeping for every mistake he'd ever made and for everything that had ever gone wrong; for the times he was to blame, and for the things that were really no one's fault but still cried out to be forgiven. At some point he understood that he was weeping not just for his daughter but for himself. He'd burdened Darcy with fear because he himself had been afraid to seize his life, to truly claim it, to embrace and honor it as his one great chance. He'd taught her to disbelieve in happiness because he'd failed to take care of his own. He hadn't recognized contentment when it was right there in front of him. He hadn't given it its proper value. He hadn't understood that happiness itself was the adventure that surpassed all others.

Hovering at his daughter's bedside, he apologized, and apologized again. He'd meant to do better; he really had. At every moment he would have fixed things if he'd only known how. But that was in the past. Now Darcy had to fix things on her own. Her father whispered in her ear that she could do it. She could seize her life, shuck off old hurts and doubts, and make a bold and flying grab at happiness. Boldness—that's what was called for. He lingered near her pillow and told her over and over that she could do it.

Wan daylight filtered into Darcy's bedroom. She twitched and blinked herself awake.

She woke up smiling and she didn't quite know why; she'd felt wretched when she went to sleep, angry with herself, hopeless. Somehow in the night her spirit had climbed up from the mat and started fighting back. She made coffee and sipped it as she looked out the window.

The morning was misty and dim; strangely, perhaps, this lifted rather than damped her mood. There was excitement in the stacked up clouds. From deep inside them, lightning did not so much flash as wink. Even as she watched, the clouds burgeoned and expanded, puffing out their chests like strutting bullies, stretching taller, arching forward.

Darcy's father, hovering near her shoulder, felt his energy waning, saw colors starting to fade as his time was running out. Summoning the last of his concentration, he whispered silently, *Remember the name of those clouds? We used to look at them in picture books. That was because they almost never happen here. Cumulonimbus. You always thought it was a funny word to say. Also known as anvil-tops. You knew that word before you had any idea what an anvil was. Remember?*

Darcy remembered, and started to smile. The smile stalled as she recalled what else she knew about those clouds. They were disaster clouds, the carriers of vicious winds and lightning strikes, of wracking spasms of flooding rain and shredding hail. Sucking vapor from the ocean, they lumbered ashore like blind giants and exploded like pricked balloons when they collided with the hills, spewing sometimes fire, sometimes ice.

Darcy put her coffee down. She paced the room for a few short moments, though she already knew what she was going to do. It was risky; it was headlong; it was very bold. She didn't know if she was wanted, if she'd be welcomed or sent away, but she had to take the chance. She threw some clothes on, grabbed her car keys and a rain jacket, and headed up to Ballard Canyon.

41.

Manny poured the tea. His hand was trembling. He felt terribly shy. He couldn't figure out where or how to start. Finally, he said, "It was wonderful to hear you play again. You play so beautifully."

Emma smiled and pointed a finger. "And you play like Manny. No one else plays quite like you."

He took it as a compliment. "You know, for a while I played better. Pretty perfectly, in fact. Not sure how it happened. But I didn't enjoy it nearly as much."

"I wouldn't have enjoyed it either. Hearing it, I mean. I love the way you play. No one puts more joy in it."

"Even in the sad parts, right? There's joy in the sad parts, too." She nodded to that. He reached across the table and touched her hand. For a moment he stroked the back of it as attentively as a blind man seeing with his fingertips, then he let his own hand rest on hers. They stayed that way for a while.

"Manny," Emma said at last, "I have to ask you something. Don't be offended. I just have to ask you. When we broke up, did you ever wonder if maybe it was because we just didn't love each other enough?"

Manny pursed his lips and thought it over. "No," he said. "I never thought of it like that. We loved each other plenty."

"Then why—?"

"We were young. Young people, I think, they have this feeling that their lives haven't really started yet. Like the real beginning is always just a little bit farther up ahead. We did what we had to do to convince ourselves that our lives had really started. You know, the grownup thing. Graduating, getting jobs."

"But if we'd really been meant to be together--?"

"What? What could have been different? You needed to do music. You really had a gift. Me? Maybe I should have followed you east and just done something else. Would the world have missed one more guy sawing away in the middle of the second fiddle section?

Maybe I would have been just as happy selling shoes or something and playing like an amateur on the weekends. And being with you. But by the time I started seeing it that way, you were married to someone else."

Very gently, Emma said, "I can't apologize for that. I had a family. I'm not sorry."

"Please, don't misunderstand. I'm happy for the life you had. I'm not even jealous. I just wish it had been with me. Wait—I guess that means I *am* jealous. But not angry. You know what I mean."

She laughed. The laughter moved the curl that came exactly halfway down her ear. "I always know what you mean, Manny. Sooner or later."

He looked down at the table. He picked up the pot to pour more tea, then realized that their first cups were still untouched. He cleared his throat and said, "So, what about now?"

Instead of answering, she said, "Do I look very young to you?"

"Very young. Very pretty. And in the dress I've always remembered."

"You look very young to me."

"I do?" He really hadn't noticed how he looked.

"Don't expect that it'll stay like this."

"Excuse me?"

"This looking young. Feeling young. It's a very temporary deal, just a way of remembering, of getting reacquainted. I don't want to mislead you. I don't want you to imagine it'll last."

"Good."

"Good?"

"Being young is what screwed us up the first time. Enough with being young. So you're saying, even here, we'll age?"

She nodded. "We'll get gray. We'll get creaky. Our skins will loosen and sometimes we'll be sick. We won't stay kids, Manny, and we won't stay young and frisky lovers. You sure you want to go through that with me?"

He didn't hesitate. "It's what I missed before. Of course I do."

She bit her lip and looked down at their nested hands. "You realize what you're saying?"

"Absolutely."

"You're saying that you want to be my mate?"

"I'm saying that I've always been your mate."

They looked at each other. They tried to smile but their features were becoming a blur of soft blue light. In the next instant, they had vanished from the green-and-white striped tent, leaving only a briefly glowing outline in the chairs where'd they been sitting.

By the time the glow had faded, they were installed in Emma's translucent room beyond the Second Membrane, and the walls had been discreetly darkened to cover their reunion.

42.

Paul DeFiore had been awake at first light, and been patrolling his vineyard since just a few minutes after. He'd been watching the weather and he was worried sick. He knew what morning overcast looked like; it was silver, it had a certain sparkle. This was altogether different. These clouds were pulpy, wet as the inside of plums; they swallowed up light and gave back only a faint and oily gleam, and they were surging up and across the coastal hills like an invading army.

In the face of their threat, Paul felt he could do nothing except what he'd seen his father do before him. He could watch over. He could put in the time. He could do small things—pull weeds, rebuild mounds of stones—token gestures that seemed to matter if only as a way of earning luck, earning mercy. He walked the rows and did what he could.

In a certain row, he spotted a tall and spiky weed that he would have sworn wasn't there the day before. Sometimes they sprouted like that, overnight; still, this was an impressive, nasty-looking thing, with a hairy stem as thick as Paul's thumb. He bent to pull it up; it didn't budge. He tried again without success. He squatted down but couldn't find the leverage. Finally he knelt, his head bent low so that the blood rushed to it and put fireworks behind his eyes. Slightly dizzy from the effort, he pulled with all his might, and finally the roots let go, abruptly, so that he rolled backwards on the damp ground and clunked his head against a wooden post.

That was when he saw his father.

The dead man's image was by no means complete. Mostly it was a suggestion of thick and bandy legs and a back that was broad but bent from decades of labor. But the voice was utterly familiar. "Hello, Paul."

"Pop?"

"Place looks great," the voice went on. "You've really been busting your hump on it."

Paul said nothing, just recalled the cadence of his father's speech. Frank DeFiore, determined to fit in and prove himself as good as anyone, had worked hard to shed his old country accent. Word by word he'd done it; but between the words there was a music that was unmistakably Italian.

"This row we're in," his father said. "Pretty sure it's where I had my heart attack."

Paul thought and may have said, "Pulling weeds?"

"Nah, hammering a post. But what I was doing just then, it didn't matter. I'd been killing myself for years. Something had to happen."

Paul shifted slightly on the moist ground where he sat with his legs straight out in front of him.

"But listen, I didn't come to talk about my heart attack. I came to say I'm sorry."

At first this didn't register. Paul wasn't sure he'd ever heard his father use that word. "Sorry?"

"Let me tell you something. Since I've been dead, looking down here, listening in, there's something I've noticed. You brag about me a lot. My old man did this, my old man said that. That used to make me feel really good. Proud. But then I started hearing something else in it. You know what I think? I think you brag about me so you won't have to admit you're mad at me."

"But I'm not—"

"I think you are, Paul. It's okay, I don't blame you. Our last conversation—you remember it?"

Of course he remembered. Pretty much every word. *Take care of your mother. Take care of the vines. Finish what I started. It's all on you now.*

"I've been thinking about that conversation."

"For seven years?" thought Paul.

"What can I say? I think slow. I'm a stubborn man. But even where I was, I was never really at peace. It took me a long time to be able to admit I was wrong."

"Wrong?"

"I shouldn't have said those things. It was selfish. Thing is, I was pissed off that I was dying. I wasn't ready. Everything I hoped to do, I'd only done it halfway yet. So I tried to stick you with it. I told myself I was giving you something. But I wasn't. Not really. I was taking something from you. I tried to steal your life so mine wouldn't end. That was wrong. I'm asking you to forgive me for that."

"There's nothing to forgive," thought Paul.

"Yes there is," his father insisted. "Come on. I'm being honest. I need to get this out there. So do you."

Paul said nothing, just leaned his head against the wooden post.

"So, couple of things," his father went on. "Your mother. My wife. She's a strong woman. Stronger than you think. Maybe stronger than I thought, too. I put it on you to take care of her. But you know what? She thinks she's taking care of you."

Paul almost laughed. "But that's—"

"That's what? Her and me, we talk, remember? I'm not saying she's right and I'm not saying she's wrong. But that's the way she sees it. She hangs around all day in case you need something. So back off a little. Let her do more on her own. Let her look to friends. It'll be better for both of you.

"Now," the visitor went on, "about the wine. I can't believe you haven't noticed this, so I'm guessing you just don't want to admit it: You're a way better winemaker than I ever was. You know what you're doing. Me, I was just a guy who threw grapes in a barrel and hoped for the best. You've passed me by. I'm fine with that. So do things your own way. You want to change things, change them. It's your place, Paul. These years since I've been gone, you've more than paid it off with sweat and caring. By now you really own it."

Paul blinked and watched the spray of fireworks behind his eyes.

"And one last thing," his father said. "This new woman you've been seeing. Excuse me for meddling, but you're giving up way too fast."

"But she lied to me, Pop."

"She made a mistake. People do. Your mother and me, you think we didn't do some dumb things, hurt each other's feelings now and then? How else do you figure things out, really get to know somebody? Besides, she wanted to explain. Why didn't you let her?"

Paul drew his legs up and hugged his knees as he considered that.

His father said, "I think maybe you were just as glad to have an out. Not to complicate your busy life. But trying to love someone, that's not a complication. That's the heart and the guts of it. The complication is all the other stuff."

Paul sat up higher, scratched his back against the wooden post. He gave his neck a tentative twist and gingerly touched the small lump on the back of his head. He tried to speak but his mouth was cottony, as though he hadn't spoken yet that day.

By the time he rose up from the ground, the image of the visitor with the broad back and bandy legs had become the merest shimmer, and the familiar sound of his father's voice had merged back into the rich quiet of the morning.

43.

On Ballard Canyon Road, between larger and more famous vineyards, a simple wooden sign marked the turnoff for the DeFiore Winery.

Following this narrow byway, Darcy drove past a rank of peeling eucalyptus trees and came to a small stucco house with an orange tile roof. By the time she parked, her windshield was streaked with rivulets of mist and yellow pollen carried on the swirling winds. Her rain jacket was soon beaded with the damp that seemed to come from everywhere.

Walking quickly, almost jogging, she moved past the winery and up into the vineyard. She saw Paul well before he'd noticed her. He was wearing faded jeans and a corduroy shirt that did not seem equal to the impending weather. He'd resumed his work by then, piling rocks, retying canes. After each small task, his eyes flicked upward toward the threatening sky. The sky seemed to be pressing down on him, hunching his neck, rounding his shoulders.

She'd come quite close before he noticed her. Immersed in his chores, still puzzling over the apparition he'd just seen, or thought he had, he missed a beat in understanding how odd but wonderful it was that she was there. All he could manage by way of greeting was to say her name.

She couldn't tell if his tone was welcoming or not. She didn't know if he was still angry. At that moment she couldn't let it matter. "I came to help," she said.

"Help?" He repeated the word rather numbly, as if its meaning somehow eluded him. Except at harvest time, he'd always worked the vineyard alone. He'd seen it as his birthright and his sole responsibility. Had he been too stubborn to share the burden or had it simply never occurred to him that it could be shared?

Rather than speak again, Darcy nodded toward the sky. The towering and inky clouds were looming closer; purple galls emerged and pulsed obscenely at their edges. From deep inside the towers, the first low growls of thunder could be heard.

Paul said, "I'm not sure I've ever seen a cloud like that."

"I have. Weatherman's daughter, remember? Could be hail, crazy wind. Is there a way to cover up the vines?"

Hands on hips, Paul looked out across his family property. The rising breeze pushed scurrying ghosts of fog in front of it. Frail green leaves stretched out from their stems like tiny flags. "It's six acres. It'll take all day."

"We could start, at least."

Paul bit his lip and considered. "Bird netting," he said at last. "Not sure it'll help much if it's hail. But maybe. Worth a shot."

Once the decision had been taken, fretting gave way to fierce but calming activity. Paul ran to the back of the winery and opened a wide-swinging door. Inside was a small tractor and, in a bin closed off with plywood, a tangled heap of the fine black mesh used to keep birds from stealing ripe grapes in the fall. He grabbed huge, wispy armfuls of the netting and loaded them onto the tractor. Darcy climbed onto the seat next to him and they clattered upslope to the highest part of the vineyard.

Putting on the netting was a kind of dance. Darcy would pull a swath of mesh out of the pile, untangling it from others, her fingers searching for edges. Paul approached her, as in a minuet, their hands briefly touching as they exchanged corners of the cloth. They backed away to the full length of the netting, sent a signal with their eyes, then bowed as they draped the mesh over a quivering vine.

The purple clouds rose up more steeply. The thunder rumbled louder, the growling punctuated now and then by sharp percussive cracks. For a while they worked without speaking; the work itself was conversation. There was intimacy in their nods, the matched rhythm of their steps and bending. Settling yet another blanket of netting on another row of vines, Paul finally said, "I haven't even thanked you."

Without looking up, Darcy said, "No need."

"But there is. Thanks for being here."

She met his gaze just for an instant and went back to the pile of netting in the tractor.

The mist changed to rain, light and threadlike at first, blowing sideways. Lightning flickered in the feeble daylight and made the air smell blue. They'd covered one small corner of the vineyard.

They pressed on. Hurry and fatigue made Darcy's fingers less nimble; she struggled with knots and snarls in the netting. After a time, the wind stopped quite suddenly, replaced by a clenched and uneasy calm. The rain grew heavier, though the fat drops fell lazily, as if swinging under parachutes. Darcy's thick hair was dampened into streaming bundles; Paul's shirt was blotched with rain at first, then uniformly darkened across his shoulders and down his spine. He wrestled with big billows of the mesh; corners of it dragged on the streaming ground and grew heavy with mud and stones.

Their pace slowed. They were sodden, overwhelmed. Just for a moment, Darcy leaned back to rest against the tractor. Paul reached out and brushed the hair from her forehead. He hadn't known he was about to do that; it happened as naturally as if he was touching his own face. They soon got back to work.

Lightning flared; thunder built and roared. The rain grew denser, tapered off, clattered down again. Then it changed to hail. The hail was more gray than white, the consistency of rock salt. Paul felt its sting against his neck and grew sick in the pit of his stomach. But the pellets were bouncing and melting against the shield of mesh. He and Darcy shrouded another row of vines, not daring to look up at the sky.

If they had looked up, they would have seen something that might perhaps have struck them as a miracle. The disastrous cloud was beginning to break down. The grim overhang of its anvil top was thinning out and stretching away like a shredded awning. The nodes and galls that had throbbed and thundered seemed to be shrinking down within themselves. Like a bully confronted, the cloud seemed to be losing its swagger, renouncing its menace.

Intent on their efforts, Paul and Darcy did not at first notice the very gradually brightening sky. Even after the hail had softened again into rain, and the rain had slacked to a caressing drizzle, they hesitated to believe that the danger was over. They trudged from row to row across the vineyard, sometimes half-leaning, half-slipping against each other as they labored against the slope.

Finally, either from sheer exhaustion or by an inspiration whose source she would never fully understand, Darcy stopped in her tracks and looked up. She sensed something that she couldn't yet see. On legs that ached but somehow felt refreshed, she bounded up the hillside to a rocky outcrop that afforded a view beyond the valley rim to the west. Standing on the small plateau, she peered as intently as a sailor seeking harbor, then windmilled her arms, shouting to Paul to join her.

Soaking wet, his shirt glued to his skin, he climbed up and stood beside her. In the distance they could see the far edge of the dying cloud, its flat and placid remnants dropping only a thin curtain of rain until it tailed away to nothing. Beyond it, a ribbon of blue sky was growing wider every moment.

Giddy with relief and fatigue, Paul started to laugh. It was a laugh that was first cousin to sobbing, a pure letting go that squeezed forth from deep in his chest. His legs went soft and he found himself sitting on the wet ground. Darcy sat down next to him, their sides nearly touching. They looked down at the vineyard, half-shrouded in billows and tangles of netting.

Still laughing, Paul said, "It'll take days to get that off again."

Darcy shrugged inside her jacket, then said, "You must be freezing."

"I'm fine," he said, but as his body quieted he was starting to shiver.

She put an arm around his shoulder. The gesture emboldened her to speak. "Can we talk about the other night?"

She felt him tighten when she said this. He couldn't help it. But this time he answered, "Only if you want to."

"I do want to. What I did, it was stupid. I'm sorry. It meant nothing. I did it because I was afraid."

"Afraid?"

"Of liking you too much. I did from the start. But what if I was wrong? It scared me."

Paul looked away a moment. "Scared me too." He plucked at the front of his wet shirt. "You at least knew you were scared. Me, I wasn't quite sure what I was."

They sat. Their sides were pressing together now; they swayed just slightly in the warm drizzle that had lightened almost into mist again. Darcy held her hand out, palm up toward the sky. "Hey, it's raining."

Paul topped her hand with his own. "Yeah, it still is."

Darcy pushed a bundle of wet hair back from her forehead. "Do you think maybe we could go inside?"

44.

With a firm though insubstantial hand, Sheila Barnett pulled her former husband away from the viewer with the lumpy green-painted base and the hammered aluminum smiley face. "Don't you think some privacy is called for?"

Very reluctantly, Hugh moved away from the device. "I just want to make sure they're okay," he said.

In truth, though, it wasn't only his daughter he yearned to keep looking at. He wished he could prolong his view of the whole blue world, the subtle sky, the rain. Now that his visits to Earth were finished, he was losing all that yet again, and it struck him as very, very beautiful.

Pulling him out of his thoughts, Sheila said, "They're fine now. You did well. You really did."

He shrugged with a pretended modesty. "Got the forecast wrong as usual. I was imagining a mini-Armageddon. What did we get? An above average thunderstorm with one little sneeze of hail."

His ex gave him a long, appraising glance. "You don't really want to talk about the weather, do you?"

He looked down at his feet and admitted that he didn't.

She waited him out, her mild glow pulsing just slightly, almost like a heartbeat.

"What I'm trying to figure," he said at last, "is why I feel so lousy. I mean, I'm happy for Darcy. I like to think I helped. And I could just sit down and cry."

"You're grieving," Sheila said. "For yourself. It's only natural."

"I guess. But there's also something besides that. I can't quite put my finger on it."

"How about vanity?"

"At this stage of the game?"

"Yeah. Wounded vanity because Darcy doesn't need you anymore. Not in the same way, at least. She'll miss you. Like she misses me. But she'll manage. We're gone, her life goes right along."

"But isn't that how—?"

"How it works? How it's meant to be? Sure. That doesn't mean it doesn't hurt. Even here, even now. You may have noticed that life is less than perfect. Why would death be different?"

Barnett toed the lawn and considered various cases of life's imperfection. Kids grew up, parents grew old. Under-standing came too late or not at all. It was the same with marriages. So many ways to mess it up. Right person, wrong attitude. Right attitude, wrong partner. Or just plain unlucky timing.

This made him think of Manny, and he asked his former wife if she'd had any news of him.

Matter of factly, Sheila said, "Emma came and got him."

"Came and got him? Just like that?"

"There was nothing *just like that* about it. He waited sixty years. She hid him in her heart while she lived a whole different life. I'd say it was a pretty damn gradual courtship. In fact, you could almost say that every single thing that went before was leading up to the moment when she came to get him."

"Wait a second," said Barnett. "Everything was leading up? Her whole life? His whole life? What was that, a warm-up?"

Sheila stood her ground. "It's possible to look at it that way. That's all I'm saying."

"But—"

"Look, there's a cockiness that goes with being alive. People think their little span on Earth is all that matters, the only real deal. Anything else is a fantasy, a fairy tale. Well, what makes them so sure? What lets them be so smug about it? Maybe life is the fantasy and *this* is the real deal. Who's to say? You can't prove it one way or the other. Anyway, Emma and Manny, they're together now."

Barnett fell back a step and took a long moment to sort through his thoughts. He was happy for Manny. He couldn't deny that he was also envious. "So," he said. "Darcy and Paul. Manny and Emma. I guess that just leaves us."

"Please, Hugh, don't start with the us stuff again."

Perhaps he should have expected that reply, but he didn't. It hurt his feelings. When he spoke again, he worked hard at not whining. "You still haven't forgiven me," he said. It was not a question.

Not unkindly, Sheila said, "Have you forgiven yourself?"

Barnett looked at the ground and thought about it. His transgressions—in themselves, they mostly just seemed trivial and childish now, more silly and embarrassing than knavish. But that didn't undo the pain he'd caused his wife and daughter. Why had he allowed himself to do that?

"Have I forgiven myself?" he repeated. "Not altogether. No. I'm working on it."

"Well, there you have it," she said. "I'm working on it, too."

Barnett looked out across the boundless lawn. He knew that it was filled with other presences, but it was so rare to find a friend, or even to encounter a fellow penitent at the diving board. He feared a loneliness that would not end. "Well, maybe, in the meantime—"

"In the meantime, what?"

"This soul mate thing. Maybe we could try it out, at least."

"Try? No, Hugh. Life is where you try. Here you do something or you don't. There's no in between, no divorces, no escape clause. You've got to be really, really sure."

Barnett's voice got very soft, almost strangled. "So you're saying we'll never be together?"

"I didn't say that."

He jumped an octave. "You didn't?"

"I said I'm not sure. Look, you're working on forgiveness, I'm working on forgiveness. If either of us ever gets there, probably both of us will. But we're not there yet."

"But how can we—?"

"I'll come visit you. We'll talk. Like now. Time isn't a problem. Besides, I like it that you're wooing me. Been ages since you've done that. So we'll take it nice and slow. Have some laughs, see what happens."

Barnett said, "Sounds a lot like dating."

"You could look at it that way."

The weatherman shook his head. "I'm dead and I'm dating my ex-wife. What a universe. Who knew?"

"I'm going for now," said Sheila, and, gradual as a summer dusk, she began to fade.

Barnett squinted to see her for as long as he could—the unruly russet hair, the suggestion of a warm soft shoulder. Then she was gone, and he was standing alone in the perfect silence of the lawn, dimly sensing the millions of others teeming past, slippery and supple as schools of silver fish.

45.

Snug and warm in the loft apartment, Darcy pulled the quilt up close beneath her chin, and said, "I love it here. It smells like wine."

Paul craned his neck above the pillow, briefly closed his eyes, and sniffed the air. "I'm here so much," he said, "sometimes I forget to notice. But, yeah, it's a delicious smell. The angels' share."

"Angels' share?"

"That's what the French call it. It's the wine that evaporates right through the barrels. Very thrifty, the French. Can't stand to see good wine go to waste. So they say it's for the angels."

Darcy propped herself on an elbow. Her thick hair flowed down in bundles across her collarbone. "And you believe it?"

"That wine shouldn't go to waste? Absolutely."

"No, the angel part."

He hesitated. He wasn't feeling coy, exactly, but…angels? He wasn't sure he was ready to buy into that sort of thing. True, something rather uncanny had happened to him that very morning. But probably it was just a passing dizzy spell that had made him imagine he was seeing his father, hearing his voice; probably it was just a clunk on the head that lowered his resistance and made him think about a few things differently.

Cautiously, he said, "Like, harps? Wings? I don't think so. Then again, who knows? This used to be my father's vineyard. If he's getting some of the wine, I guess that's nice."

"My folks, too," said Darcy. "Save a glass for them." She traced out his eyebrows with a fingertip. "Your Dad, how long's he been gone?"

"Seven years."

"My mother's been dead for nine. Seems like a long time, doesn't it?"

Paul stroked her hair as he considered that. "Yes and no. Sometimes I can hardly remember when my father was alive. I mean, I remember him. It's my own life that seems so different." He paused and looked past Darcy's shoulder. "Other times it feels like he was here this morning."

"Or every morning," she said. "Sometimes, with my Mom, my father too all of a sudden, I have this funny feeling, like they haven't really left at all."

Shying from the subject, Paul said, "Maybe all of us should do a tasting. Have some cheese and crackers, maybe?"

"Okay, make fun. I don't mind. But I mean it. Not like ghosts or magic wands or anything like that. Maybe it's just a different way of saying memories. Everyone has memories, right?"

"Right. Sure. But they're in the past. They're done."

"Are they?" Darcy said. "That's the part I'm not so sure about. Memories just sit there? Finished? That isn't how it feels to me. I think memories keep changing. At least their meaning does. You move forward, your memories move forward, too. You change, they change. If they're part of you, how could they not?"

Paul said nothing. Grateful for the feel of her skin, he ran his hand along her back.

"Like this morning," she went on. "I woke up and I knew I would come here. I didn't know that when I went to sleep. What happened? Did I dream it? Maybe. But to me it was more like a memory showed a different side. The past changed. Or at least that's how it felt."

She shrugged. It was a leisurely, luxurious, yawning sort of shrug that moved the ripples in the quilt and nestled her more deeply in the crook of Paul's arm. Quiet now, they drank in the winey air and looked across the loft apartment to a window that faced out toward the vineyard. The sky had cleared and wisps of mist were rising from the wet but warming ground. The steady weather was already settling in again, promising many days of mild temperatures, sunshine with some morning fog and passing clouds, and a light breeze off the ocean.

About the Author

Laurence Shames has been a New York City taxi driver, lounge singer, furniture mover, lifeguard, dishwasher, gym teacher, and shoe salesman. Having failed to distinguish himself in any of those professions, he turned to writing full-time in 1976 and has not done an honest day's work since.

His basic laziness notwithstanding, Shames has published more than twenty books and hundreds of magazine articles and essays. Best known for his critically acclaimed series of Key West novels, he has also authored non-fiction and enjoyed considerable though largely secret success as a collaborator and ghostwriter. Shames has penned four New York Times bestsellers. These have appeared on four different lists, under four different names, none of them his own. This might be a record.

From 1999 to 2013, Shames lived in Southern California and pretended to be in the movie business. *THE ANGELS' SHARE* is the first novel he has set on the West Coast.

He currently divides his year between Asheville, NC and Naples, FL.

For more information, please visit http://www.laurenceshames.com.

Works by Laurence Shames

Key West Novels—
Tropical Swap
Shot on Location
The Naked Detective
Welcome to Paradise
Mangrove Squeeze
Virgin Heat
Tropical Depression
Sunburn
Scavenger Reef
Florida Straits

Key West Short Fiction—
Chickens

New York and California Novels—
Money Talks
The Angels' Share

Nonfiction—
The Hunger for More
The Big Time

47470288R00109

Made in the USA
San Bernardino, CA
06 April 2017